What's French for HELP, George?

What's French for HELP, George?

Helen McCann
Illustrated by Ellen Eagle

Aitken, George
Papillon sur Mer

SIMON & SCHUSTER BOOKS FOR YOUNG READERS

Published by Simon & Schuster
New York • London • Toronto • Sydney • Tokyo • Singapore

Also by Helen McCann:
What Do We Do Now, George?

 SIMON & SCHUSTER BOOKS FOR YOUNG READERS
Simon & Schuster Building, Rockefeller Center, 1230 Avenue of the Americas,
New York, New York 10020. Text copyright © 1990 by Helen McCann.
Illustrations copyright © 1993 by Ellen Eagle. All rights reserved including
the right of reproduction in whole or in part in any form. Originally published
in Great Britain by Simon & Schuster Young Books. First U.S. Edition 1993.
SIMON & SCHUSTER BOOKS FOR YOUNG READERS
is a trademark of Simon & Schuster.

Designed by David Neuhaus.
Manufactured in the United States of America   10   9   8   7   6   5   4   3   2   1

Library of Congress Cataloging-in-Publication Data. McCann, Helen. What's
French for help, George? / by Helen McCann ; illustrated by Ellen Eagle.   p.   cm.
Summary: With the reluctant help of his friends, thirteen-year-old, trouble-prone
George manages to win a free ticket for the school trip to France, where his
well-meaning ideas cause the usual commotion.   [1. School excursions—Fiction.
2. Friendship—Fiction.   3. France—Fiction.]   I. Eagle, Ellen, ill.   II. Title
PZ7.M1244W1   1993   [Fic]—dc20   CIP   91–41563   ISBN 0–671–74689–8

For my nephew Malcolm

Aitken, George
Papillon sur Mer

George skulked behind the partition, listening. He felt like a spy, but what else could he do? They wouldn't talk about it when he was around. "They" were Stick, Tub, Kev, and Julia. George had been friends with Kev, Stick, and Tub for years—as long as he could remember, since grade school at least, so he knew them pretty well. This was the first time he had ever known them not to talk about what was on their minds.

It was Julia's fault, of course. Julia was Stick's eleven-year-old sister and, whereas Stick was like an elongated drumstick, Julia was tiny. The two-year difference in their ages didn't account for it. As far as growing went in Stick's family, he had cornered the market. Julia was the one who wouldn't let them talk about it when George was around. They thought they were being sensitive, but all they were doing was making George mad. All except Kev. Kev couldn't be sensitive if you paid him. He'd started to say something about it the other day, but Julia had grabbed him by the logo on his T-shirt and stabbed him in the ribs with her finger. She was growing her nails. Sensitive!

"Shut up, Kev," she said, nearly breaking her neck looking up at him.

"Eh?" said Kev, which was what Kev mainly said when you spoke to him.

Kev was built like a wedge—a big wedge and solid.

"I said, shut up, Kev," said Julia, giving him another stab with the talon.

"I only wanted to show you my passport photo," Kev said.

George had looked at it. "Good likeness, Kev," he said.

Kev grinned. "Thanks, George."

George shook his head. Kev really did seem pleased. People were strange.

"You can sell passports for a fortune," Tub said through a mouthful of jelly beans. "My mom says it's a disgrace." They all tried to think of something

Tub's mom didn't think was a disgrace. Tub looked at the photo again. "Well, maybe not."

Julia changed the subject by reminding Stick that he had to take the dog to the vet. Stick began to tremble. Stick was a good guy, but where Julia and the dog were concerned, the only word to describe him was *craven*. The dog was tiny as well. Maybe that was it. Small things. Like elephants being afraid of mice.

That had been the other day and Julia had kept them firmly off the topic ever since, at least whenever George was around. He continued to skulk behind the partition, reading the graffiti and listening at the same time. It wasn't difficult. The graffiti wasn't very clever. But neither was the conversation. He sighed. Somebody had tried to spell *assassinate* three times and had eventually written "sleigh." He drew a picture of a Christmas tree beside it with a felt-tipped pen. It was the responsibility that weighed so heavily on him. They weren't fit to be let loose without him. They would probably end up being deported.

He chose a crack in the partition, clamped an eye to it, and his breathing went funny. Sharon Taylor always did that to him. Long blond hair and eyes like lasers. She had only one fault—apart from a tendency to bossiness and talking funny and being so good at everything—and that was not being able to see George's good points. He couldn't understand it. He'd even worn tights for her once to play in *Romeo and Juliet* at school. Admittedly, it hadn't been a total success, but he'd made the effort. Sharon drifted up to them just as Stick was showing Tub where the dog had bitten him when he took it to the vet.

"Why are you rolling your pant leg up, Paul?"

Sharon always called people by their real names.

"I'm showing him my scar," said Stick.

Tub was looking puzzled. "How did it get that high? It's just a little dog."

"It sort of leapt up and hung on," said Stick.

"What did you do to it?"

"Tried to get it off. What do you think?" said Stick.

"No, I mean before it attacked you?"

"Nothing," said Stick. "I was only taking it to the vet."

Tub rolled a candy around his teeth. "Must have sensed it," he said. "Animals are like that. Extrasensory perception, they call it, ESP. And they don't like going to the vet." He crunched the candy. "Must be like going to the dentist." Tub went to the dentist a lot.

"You shouldn't eat so many sweets, Philip," Sharon said.

Tub looked at her for a moment before he realized she was talking to him. "Oh, sorry. Want one?" he said, holding out a paper bag.

Sharon ignored the bag, but Tub didn't get annoyed. Tub hardly ever got annoyed.

Sharon looked around the group. Tub, Stick, Kev, and Julia. Tub was the only one who wasn't actually glowering. Kev's eyebrows were drawn together in a straight line, making him look even more like a gorilla with a toothache than usual. Julia's chin was stuck out at a belligerent angle, and Stick was doubled up, still holding his pant leg and giving a passable impression of a bent pin. The only thing George and the rest of them disagreed about absolutely all the time was Sharon Taylor. Mostly they just pitied him and said he'd grow out of it.

"I only came to tell you there's a meeting about the trip at two o'clock in the school auditorium," Sharon said.

Julia nearly smiled. "Great, I've got math," she said. "Bet I know what it's about."

"What?" said Kev.

"Wait and see," Julia said smugly.

Sharon gave her a look—lasers in action. "Are you going?"

Julia squared up to her. "Why shouldn't I be going?"

Sharon looked at Stick, and he unfolded himself and stood up. "Don't blame me," he said. "Mom said if Julia couldn't go, I wasn't going either. She says she and Dad are going to have the best vacation ever."

Tub crunched. "Where are they going?"

"Nowhere," said Stick.

"I thought you said they were going to have the best vacation ever."

"They are," said Stick. "Staying at home without us."

Tub looked thoughtful. "You'll probably be scarred for life."

Stick bent over and rolled his pant leg back down. "I'll bet I am," he said.

"Not the dog," Tub said. "Your mom and dad, rejecting you like that."

"What about you, then?" said Stick. "How come you aren't rejected?"

"They said it was educational," said Tub.

Kev untangled his eyebrows. "My dad said if I didn't go, he'd cut my allowance for six months, social worker or no social worker."

Kev was always talking about his social worker, trying to make them jealous. He had gotten one when he'd chained himself to some trees to prevent their being chopped down, and had to be cut loose by the fire department. Once he got the social worker, there was no way he was letting her go again. She was really in favor of an allowance.

"Don't you feel rejected?" said Tub.

"What do you mean?" said Kev.

"Your dad wanting you out of his hair."

Kev thought for a moment. You could see it happening. "My dad always wants me out of his hair."

"Your social worker's going on the school trip," said Julia.

Usually nobody argued with Julia. She was a real pest, always tagging along, but she always seemed to know what was going on. Sometimes she seemed to know before it had even happened. She wanted to be a reporter when she grew up. Sharon wasn't as used to her as the rest of them were, not that it would have made too much difference to Sharon.

"Don't be silly, Julia. Only teachers are allowed to go."

"They couldn't get enough," said Julia, "so Mr. Martin got Jenny to say she would go."

Mr. Martin was George's French teacher and Jenny was Kev's social worker—and Mr. Martin's girlfriend.

Sharon narrowed her eyes and the lasers homed in on Kev. "I wonder why they couldn't get enough teachers to go," she said. Kev didn't notice.

"The dog isn't," said Stick. "That's one good thing about this trip."

"Isn't what?" said Tub.

"Going," said Stick. "It isn't allowed. Rabies."

"That's just for dogs coming into this country," said Sharon.

Panic showed on Stick's face. "Don't tell Mom, or

she'll want me to take the dog as well as Julia," he said, and ducked automatically. It didn't work. Ducking only gave Julia a better target.

"The dog would have to spend six months in quarantine when it got back," said Sharon. "Not that the school would let you take it anyway."

Stick was suddenly paying attention as well as rubbing the side of his head. "Six months?"

"Mr. Martin wouldn't let you take the dog," said Tub.

"Mr. Martin wouldn't know," said Stick. "Six months without the dog!"

Sharon was looking at him.

"Only a joke, Sharon," said Stick.

"I certainly hope so," said Sharon severely. "It would be very irresponsible to try to take a dog out of the country like that."

"I wish you wouldn't talk like that, Sharon," he said.

"My mom says we'll get all sorts of things running through the Channel tunnel," said Tub. "She says it isn't safe."

"What's quarantine?" said Kev.

"It's like when you get chicken pox and have to stay home from school," said Julia absentmindedly. She was looking at Stick as well.

"The dog doesn't go to school," said Kev.

"Rats and moles and all kinds of things," Tub was saying. "Probably wolves as well."

"What?" said Julia, then she rounded on Kev. "Look, Kev, forget it. Nobody's taking the dog. Right, Stick?"

"Oh, right, Julia," said Stick.

From behind the partition George caught sight of the gleam in Stick's eye, and groaned. He was right. They would end up being deported.

"Where's George?" Sharon was saying, and George almost fell through the partition in surprise.

"Who wants him?" said Kev.

Sharon ignored him. "Let him know about the meeting, will you?" she said.

"George isn't going on the trip," Stick said.

Sharon had turned on her heel, but she turned back at that. "Not going?" she said. "But you're all going. Even Julia."

"What do you mean, even me?" said Julia.

"Why isn't he going?" said Sharon.

"Hates French," said Stick.

"Gets seasick," said Tub.

"Julia won't let me ask him," said Kev.

"Julia?" said Sharon.

"Look, Sharon," said Julia. "There's only George and his mom, and his mom can't afford to send him on school trips to France, so we don't talk about it when he's around. So just don't go mentioning any meetings to him, okay?"

George peered through the crack in the partition. Sharon was standing there looking down at Julia, her blond hair drifting on her shoulders and her blue eyes looking as if they didn't understand what Julia was talking about. Julia was drawn up to her full height, which wasn't much, and her dark, curly hair was standing out on end as if electrified. He knew they meant well. Julia was the worst. Ever since she'd started taking modern studies—looking at social issues—she'd been a pain. Stick said she'd even become a vegetarian. It would wear off—he hoped. He really, honestly, knew they meant well, but he wished they wouldn't. Sensitive! They were as sensitive as a tractor-trailer.

"But he's the only one of you who has any sense," Sharon was saying. "And even he hasn't got much."

George was overcome. It was the nicest thing she'd ever said about him. He felt quite weak and he clutched at the partition for support.

He got some warning. It wobbled a bit before it fell over and crashed at Sharon's feet, so he was able to look as if he'd just been passing by.

"You can always send me a postcard, Sharon," he said.

She looked from the felt-tipped pen still in his hand to the partition at her feet. "That isn't the way you spell *slay*," she said, and walked away.

"I didn't know she could read upside down," George was saying admiringly when the rest of them attacked him.

Aitken, George
Papillon sur Mer

2

At two o'clock George was supposed to be having French, only Mr. Martin had to go to the meeting about the trip to France.

"How come you're going on this trip, sir?" George asked him as he gathered up some papers from his desk.

Mr. Martin gave him one of his patient looks. He was good at patient looks. He used them a lot.

"I'm a French teacher, George, or hadn't you noticed?"

Nobody in George's French class was very good at French.

George persisted. "I thought you did a deal with Mr. Redfeather," he said.

Mr. Martin dropped the patient look and tried suspicion. He wasn't nearly as good at suspicion. Not enough practice. Mr. Martin was okay—for a teacher.

"How did you know about that?" he said.

So it was true. George had been nearly sure he'd overheard Mr. Martin and the headmaster agreeing that Mr. Martin didn't have to take the school trip to France if he helped with fund-raising last term. The fund-raising idea had been George's—for his own purposes naturally, only it hadn't quite worked out the way he'd planned it. It had been sort of a disaster, really. In fact, a total disaster. Rumor had it that Mr. Redfeather had started marking off the days till his retirement on the calendar in his study the day after the fund-raising play—the one George had worn the tights in. Mr. Redfeather wasn't due to retire for another five years.

"Word gets around," said George. "You helped with that fund-raising."

"If I hadn't helped with the fund-raising, I'd only have to take the trip this year," said Mr. Martin. "Since I did help, I've now got to take it next year as well."

It really hadn't been a success.

"But don't think I'm blaming you, George," Mr.

Martin was saying. George thought it was time to change the subject.

"I'm not going on the trip," he said.

"There's always that," said Mr. Martin, "but the rest of your mob are."

George couldn't find anything comforting to say about that. "You'll be late for your meeting," he said.

Mr. Martin groaned. "More problems," he said.

George tried to look interested and intelligent at the same time. At least they were off the subject of who was to blame for the fund-raising fiasco.

"You all right, George?" said Mr. Martin. "You look a bit peculiar."

"Just taking an intelligent interest," said George. "What's the problem?"

"A free ticket," said Mr. Martin.

George was puzzled. Teachers were strange.

"Free isn't a problem," he said.

"It is when you've got to decide how to allocate it," said Mr. Martin. "The tour company has decided to do this promotional thing—giving away a free ticket with every trip."

"I still don't see the problem."

The patient look was back. "Look, George, we've got all these kids who have already paid. We can't just give a free ticket to someone else."

George thought for a moment. "And the ticket has to be free?"

"Yes."

"You can't just divide up the cost among the ones who are going?"

"No, it's advertising. It's got to be a free ticket."

"Ignore it," said George. "They can't make you take it. Or give it to a teacher."

Mr. Martin looked at him sadly. "We couldn't get teachers to come if we paid them. It was all done by blackmail."

"Except for Jenny," said George.

"Jenny's a social worker," said Mr. Martin. "She's got a conscience."

"And teachers don't."

"What do you think?" said Mr. Martin.

"Then, ignore it," said George again.

"We can't," said Mr. Martin. "Some of the kids have got wind of it already. They'd lynch us if we tried to ignore it."

George thought of Julia saying "Bet I know what it's about." Mr. Martin was quite right.

"Have a raffle," said George.

Mr. Martin hung his head. "If we have a raffle and somebody who has already paid wins, we still have their ticket booked and they have to get their money back, and by this stage we won't get a refund. The only thing is, I can't see what else we're going to do."

George concentrated. He was beginning to see the problem.

"It's like one of those things we do in computer class," he said. "Logic and flowcharts and stuff."

Mr. Martin looked up. "That's it!" he said. "We'll get the computer to do it. Then nobody can blame us."

George tried to appear shocked. "Don't let Mrs. Lucas hear you saying that," he said. "She's always telling us it's human error. Computers do only as they're told."

Mrs. Lucas was the computer studies teacher. Mr. Martin wasn't listening.

"Got to go, George," he said. "Thanks for the idea."

"Don't mention it," said George. His mind was beginning to work overtime. What he needed was a computer expert. His eyes roamed around the class and lit upon Chris Simmonds. Rotten at French but a computer whizkid.

"Chris," he said, "if you were writing a program to—" and he was off.

Mr. Martin had left a senior in charge of them, which was no problem. The senior put a lookout on the door, told them not to break up the furniture, and went out through the emergency exit to the fire escape for a smoke. George and Chris had a very interesting conversation, and George wished he'd paid more attention in computer class. Chris went on and on about loops and switches and IFS, THENS, and ELSES and drew flowcharts over everything that wasn't actually moving at the time. By the end of it, George was beginning to think he might stand a better chance with a straightforward raffle.

George had a philosophy of life. In fact, he had several, depending on what the problem was. In this case the problem was luck, and George's philosophy was you made your own. Besides, he had a responsibility. If he let those kids go off without him, they'd probably cause an international incident. Even Sharon had said he should be going with them, or she would have if he hadn't nearly killed her with that partition before she got the chance.

So he listened to Chris until his brain felt like spaghetti, and pocketed all the flowcharts he could. The best one was on a desktop, which was too bad.

The senior came back from his smoke and started a poker school in the corner. Chris's eyes lit up and George took the hint. As casually as he could, he said, "You going on this French trip?"

Chris looked up. "No way. I'm going on a computer immersion week."

George marveled. People really were strange. Still, you had to be fair. You also had to suss out the opposition.

He watched Chris muscle in on the poker game. She would have the senior cleaned out in ten minutes. She had that kind of mind—computers and poker.

George copied the flowchart from the desktop, then took it down the corridor to scrub off the evidence. It was half off its hinges anyway. When he came back, Mr. Martin was there.

"What are you doing with a desktop, George?" he said.

"Art department was short of drawing boards, sir," he said. "How did the idea go?"

"Fine," said Mr. Martin. "Mention computers and people will swallow anything. About that desktop..."

The bell rang and there was a stampede. Chris bumped into George as she zoomed past. The loose change in her blazer pocket swung against his ribs. It would leave a bruise. She clanked down the corridor, listing to one side.

"You got a system, Chris?" he called after her.

She grinned back at him. "I'll draw you a flowchart."

Mr. Martin and George walked down the corridor together. "So what's the plan?" said George.

"Mrs. Lucas is going to write a program for us," said Mr. Martin. "It'll run through the names till it comes up with someone who isn't actually going but wants to."

George considered this. "Some people might say that isn't fair," he said.

"Only if they know about it," said Mr. Martin. "Do you want to talk about that desktop, George?"

"Who said life was fair?" said George.

"Anyway," said Mr. Martin, "if we put everybody into the computer, the odds are it'll come up with somebody who isn't already going. And we'll never know if we're getting its first choice or not. And it makes the administrative side easier."

That was it, thought George. If he went on this trip, it would make the administrative side easier. Mr. Martin wouldn't have all the hassle of having his mob deported. Besides, the computer thing had been his idea and Mr. Martin was all for simplicity. What could be simpler than George hacking into the computer and making sure he was the one who got the free ticket? It would make everybody's life easier. In fact, it was his duty to do it—as a responsible person. Luck? You couldn't trust it. You had to make your own. There was one small problem, but then, things were never entirely simple. He patted the pocket with the flowcharts in it. Easy!

Aitken, George
Papillon sur Mer
voir, rue de Sudon

3

The next thing George had to do was get the spy network set up. He called a meeting for that evening at the usual place in the park. Tub was there before him, sitting at the edge of the pond. The cherub, which was a fountain really but had been shut off, stood slightly askew on its base in the middle of the pond. George heaved a pebble at it. He had been stoning it into submission for years. He pinched one of Tub's fries. It tasted a bit funny.

"Your mom still got you on a diet?"

"Rabbit food," said Tub. "How can you live on rabbit food? I've told her it's my metabolism, but she won't listen. What's the meeting about?"

"The trip," said George.

Tub stopped chewing for a second. "Is Julia coming?"

There was a yelping from behind the hedge that backed onto the tennis courts, and Stick and Julia came around the corner. Stick was dragging a small black furry thing on a leash behind him.

"Walking the dog?" said Tub, and doubled his rate of fry intake before Julia could say anything.

"It's embarrassing," said Stick. "I don't know why she couldn't have gotten a real dog."

"Ignore him," said Julia. "Somebody has just asked him how many batteries it takes. What's the meeting about?"

"The trip," said George.

Julia's eyes narrowed, then a voice spoke from behind George. Kev was one of those big people who can move really silently—as long as he was in a clear space.

"What's the meeting about?" he said.

"The trip," George said for the last time. Mr. Martin wasn't the only one who could be patient.

They all started talking at once.

"I thought you weren't going," said Tub.

"Julia won't let us talk to you about it," said Stick.

"What trip?" said Kev.

George turned to Julia. "Your turn," he said.

"There's a free ticket," said Julia.

Trust Julia.

"I know," George said.

"Mrs. Lucas is going to write a computer program to pick a winner," said Tub.

"I know that too," said George. "It was my idea. Mr. Martin was going to have a raffle."

"What's wrong with a raffle?"

George chucked another stone at the cherub. "Raffles aren't logical," he said.

"You're going to fix the computer," said Julia.

It wasn't something he would ever admit, but there were times when George found himself almost grateful to Julia. She saved a lot of time.

"I'm going to modify the program," he corrected her.

Stick looked doubtful. "Last computer lesson you wiped a whole term's spreadsheet data from the disk."

"There should have been a backup disk," said George. "Anybody knows that."

"It took us weeks to key that stuff in," said Stick. "And what about the bits that kept falling off the screen?"

"Computer virus," said George. "How could anybody blame me for that? It happens all the time."

"You shouldn't be eating that rubbish," said Julia to Tub.

"They're vegetables, aren't they?" said Tub, then

turned to George. "Anyway, I don't see how you're going to fix the computer when you're banned from the computer room for the next two weeks." He finished his last fry and gave the paper to the dog. The dog started licking furiously. Tub had spotted George's small problem.

"Ah," said George.

They all froze. Even Kev got a whiff of the menace contained in that "ah."

George took advantage of the silence. "There's a computer in Mr. Martin's storage closet," he said.

"So?" said Stick.

"So, it's linked to the computer room," said George, "for him to fool around with his vocabulary programs and all."

"So?" said Stick again.

He could be really boring sometimes.

"So all I need is for one of you to get Mrs. Lucas's program onto the network in the computer room and I can hack into it from Mr. Martin's computer and work on it."

"Hacking's an expert's job," said Julia. "How can you hack into a system when you can't even work a spreadsheet program?"

"I've taken expert advice," said George.

"Oh, yeah, whose?" said Stick.

"Chris Simmonds's."

This time the silence was respectful.

"If you've got Chris Simmonds, why do you need us?" said Tub.

"Because I can't tell her exactly what I'm after," said George. "I'd be paying hush money for years."

"That's true," said Stick.

A glimmer of agreement at last. George pressed home his advantage. "Look, it's simple. All I need is to know when the program's finished and then arrange a time when one of you can feed it into the file server on the network. An idiot could do it."

"She won't let me off the old PC," said Kev.

"Who won't?" said George.

"Mrs. Lucas."

"She'll have to write it this week," said Julia.

"How come?" Tub said.

"Because she's taking a training course next week," Julia explained. "Something to do with modems." Julia knew everything.

"What's a modem?" said Kev.

"It's what you hack into computer systems with," said Julia. "It's a telephone link. The school doesn't have one." She looked at George.

"I've worked out another way," said George. "Trust me. What's happening to the computer room while she's away?"

Julia shrugged. "I suppose it'll be locked up. The classes are cancelled. Nobody else to take them."

"Chris will get withdrawal symptoms," Tub said.

"There's something wrong with the dog."

They all looked. Its tongue was hanging out of its mouth, and it was panting a lot and scrabbling at the low wall of the pond.

"It's having a heart attack," said Stick.

Julia didn't look convinced. "Do dogs get heart attacks?"

"They've got hearts, haven't they?" said Stick.

"It's cholesterol," said Tub. "My mom saw a program on television about it. That's why she won't let me eat fries."

"Doesn't seem to stop you," said Julia.

"Maybe it wants a drink," said Kev.

He lifted the dog and set it on the wall of the pond. It splayed across the wall, lapping frenziedly.

"Just thirsty," said Tub. "Must have been the salt on the paper."

"Salt can give you heart attacks," said Stick.

"No, it can't," said Julia. "They've found out salt isn't bad for you after all."

"They're always doing that," said Tub, "saying things are bad for you, then changing their minds. I guess they'll start telling us sweets are good for you soon."

"Anyway, it isn't having a heart attack," said Julia.

There was a splash as the dog fell into the water. It didn't seem to mind. It just swam around, swallowing the pond.

"That water isn't too clean," said Tub.

Stick hauled the dog out. It stood there, dripping and still panting.

"It can't still be thirsty," he said, "it's had half the pond."

The dog rolled its eyes, tongue lolling. George still had that funny taste in his mouth—a sort of burning sensation.

"Was there anything else on those fries, Tub," he asked, "besides salt?"

"Chili sauce," said Tub.

Everybody looked at Stick and waited for the outburst.

Usually he got furious if anybody so much as breathed on the dog. Now it had just had chili sauce and mucky pond water.

"It might as well get used to funny food," said Stick.

They relaxed, all except George. He was deeply suspicious, but he didn't have time to go into that with Stick now. It just proved how vital it was for him to go on this trip.

"Can we get back to business?" he said. "I need to know when the program is written, what it's called, what disk it's on, and a printout would be helpful if you can get one. Oh, and I'd like access to the data disk it'll be using."

They were all looking at him, stunned.

"Don't want much, do you?" said Stick.

"It's all this spy stuff on TV," Tub said. "My mom says it's a disgrace. Gives people ideas."

"If it gives you any ideas, it'll be a miracle," said George. "I'm depending on you all."

That shook them. They weren't used to George's depending on them. Usually it was the other way around.

"In that case, how much is it worth?" said Stick.

"How would your mom like to hear about the chili sauce?" said George.

"You can depend on me, George," said Tub. Stick's mom didn't waste time asking for explanations.

Kev grinned. "Any fixing to be done, you just ask me, George," he said.

"Thanks, Kev," said George. "I'll let you know."

Silence.

"Julia?"

"Okay."

No arguments. That wasn't like Julia.

"Just okay?" he said.

"Just okay," said Julia. "For the moment."

That didn't sound too good, but George was in no position to argue and Julia had a genius for finding things out. He was going to need her. He decided to take her at her word.

"Okay," he said, "now you can tell me all about the trip."

Once they'd started they couldn't stop talking about it. An outdoor activities center on the coast of Brittany. Sailing, windsurfing, canoeing. And he was there already—or almost. Only a few minor details to sort out. Like fixing that program.

Aitken, George
Papillon sur Mer

4

By Friday George was up to his eyes in hacking techniques. The trouble was, they all seemed to use modems—modulators/demodulators. He could have written a book on modems by now. They used telephone lines to link two computers. It was like linking two brains. Everything in one memory could be passed to the other. But as Julia had pointed out, the school didn't have modems, so he had to rely on human help, and in his case the human help wasn't all that reliable.

He had worked it out though. The only computer in the computer room that wasn't linked into the network was the old PC—the one Kev used. It was standing alone with its disk drive and printer. The rest were linked into one disk drive, the file server, and it fed programs to all the machines on the network.

Friday. His one and only chance. Mr. Martin's room was free the same period Stick and Kev had computer studies. George, being banned, had a library period. No problem. Mr. Martin never locked his room or his storage closet. As he said, "Find me a kid in this school who wants to steal a French book and I'll show you a kid who's turned up at the wrong school." He was a funny guy sometimes, Mr. Martin. George thought he would have to have a talk with him about this lack of security. He was too trusting for a teacher. He just didn't see all the possibilities.

The program was written. Julia had found that out. She had also found out what it was called and what disk it was on. She was amazing. The only thing she hadn't managed to get so far was a printout. Of course, George would have found out these things himself, but he didn't want any questions asked later about why he'd been interested. Pity it wasn't Julia's computer studies period. He had to depend on Stick. Kev wasn't allowed onto the network. He collared Stick between classes and thrust a sheet of paper at him.

"What's this?" said Stick.

"Instructions," said George. "Just follow these and it'll work like a dream."

Stick scanned the paper. "What's this about taking me over?"

"Your network station," said George. "It's simple. I get onto the network from Mr. Martin's computer and I can talk to you."

"How?" said Stick.

"On the computer screen," said George. "All I do is take over your station and type what I want you to do on my machine and it comes up on your screen. The only thing is, I need to know which station is yours, so you'll have to grab station twelve."

"How do I know which one that is?" said Stick.

George sighed. "A message comes up on the screen when you log onto the system. Station twelve is the one nearest the door. The one farthest away from Mrs. Lucas's desk."

Stick jumped. "And you think she won't notice?"

"She won't notice," said George.

"She's got eyes in the back of her head," said Stick. "Of course she'll notice."

"Not this time," said George.

"Why not?"

"Because, among other things, Kev is going to have a problem," said George. "One that's going to keep Mrs. Lucas busy."

"If it's that bad, she'll close down the whole network," said Stick.

George smiled. "She never does that and, besides, Kev isn't allowed on the network. His problem is what you might call localized. Remember—station twelve. See you. I've got to find Kev."

Stick looked at the paper in his hand. "What do you want me to do with this," he called after George. "Eat it once I've read it, or does it self-destruct?"

George grinned. "Destruction is Kev's department."

He found Kev looking miserable in a corner of the playground.

"What's up?"

"Sharon Taylor," said Kev. "She won't stop nagging me about how she expects me to stay out of trouble on the trip. Anybody would think she was in charge. She's worse than the teachers."

"Forget Sharon," said George, and thought he must be cracking up. Still, you had to get your priorities right, and right now fixing that program was number one on his list.

"Look, Kev, there's something I want you to type into your computer this afternoon."

"What?" said Kev. "I can't type very well."

George handed him a sheet of paper. "This."

Kev looked relieved. "Not much, is it? What does it do?"

"It's a surprise," said George. "Just type it in, save it, and when Stick gives you the word, run it. Only make sure you get it right, Kev. It's important."

Kev looked at it. "It's only four lines."

"Yeah," said George. "Just check them character by character and don't run it till you get the word."

"What name will I save it under?" said Kev.

George thought. He didn't think Kev could spell *apocalypse* the same way twice, or *Armageddon* or *anarchy*. Why did all the good words begin with "a"? He tried "b."

"Blowup," he said.

Kev wrote it down.

Julia next. He caught up with her just as the bell rang.

"No printout," she said before he even asked. "People have a habit of looking at what you're printing out."

George shrugged. "Have to do without it, then. What about the disk?"

"That's okay," she said. "The data is on the same disk as the program. It's in the rack with the master disks."

You had to hand it to Julia. She had her uses. Of course, you needed an organizing brain behind it all.

"What has she called the program?" he said.

Julia gave him a sideways look. "Raffle," she said.

Terrific, thought George. So Mrs. Lucas had a sense of humor.

He drifted through the rest of the morning thinking about the trip. It would be wonderful.

He got them all together for a final run-through at lunchtime.

"Right," he said. "Here's the plan."

There was a collective groan that he ignored. They always groaned when he said that.

"We give Mrs. Lucas time to set up the lesson, say ten minutes, then I log on the network and get through to you, Stick."

"And what's Mrs. Lucas going to say when you come through with stuff on my screen? You know what she's like. . . ."

"She won't be there," said George.

"Why not?" said Tub.

"Because she'll be looking after Julia," said George.

"What?" said Julia. She could make the simplest words sound threatening.

"You'll have fainted outside the computer room door, and Tub will rush in and drag Mrs. Lucas out to help."

"Forget it," said Julia.

"We need a diversion," said George. "To give Stick time to change the disk on the file server. It won't take long, and once I've got the stuff on my machine he can change it back again."

"I've never fainted in my life," said Julia, "and I'm not starting now."

"Julia," said George.

"No."

"I thought you said Kev was going to—" Stick began.

"Run a program," George cut in. "That's for later, when I have to have the disk back in the network to save the fixed program on."

"Sounds complicated," said Stick.

"It isn't," George said. "Not if you take it step by step. It's dead simple really. Step one—a diversion while you switch the disk. Step two—I get the program onto my machine. Step three—you switch the disks back. Step four—I fix the program. Step five— another diversion while you switch the disk again. Step six—I save the fixed program onto Mrs. Lucas's disk. Step seven—you switch the disk again and it's done. Dead simple."

"You call that simple?" said Stick.

"Just follow your instructions," George said. "Trust me."

"I hate it when you say that," said Stick.

"Tub, you aren't feeling well," said George.

"I'm feeling fine," said Tub. "I don't have to do any of this disk-switching stuff. I don't even have computer class this afternoon."

"No, you aren't," George said. "You're feeling

really terrible. You're going to faint. Too much candy, I guess."

They all began to shout at him, but he could stand it. He was used to it.

"What about me, George?" said Kev when they'd shouted themselves hoarse.

"Just get those four lines typed in while Mrs. Lucas is giving Tub the kiss of life," said George.

Tub made a dive at him.

"Joke," said George. "Knowing Mrs. Lucas, she'll probably pour a jug of water over you."

When the bell rang at the end of lunch period, George wasn't entirely convinced that he had a completely happy team. Nobody saw him going into Mr. Martin's classroom. He slipped in like a shadow and was quite pleased with himself till he bumped into a pile of books on Mr. Martin's desk and sent them cascading onto the floor. There was no time to pick them up. He was working on a tight schedule. He would get them later. He couldn't afford to leave any clues to show that he'd been there—that anybody had been there. Nobody seemed to have heard the books fall, or if they had, nobody took any notice. He tiptoed into the storage closet and shut the door behind him. There was Mr. Martin's computer, sitting there waiting for him—his passport to France. It was only when he was sitting in front of it that he began to feel a bit nervous. When you read about hacking and saw films about it, it all seemed to work perfectly. He took a deep breath and switched the machine on. This was it.

Five minutes later he was still trying to log on the network system. All the machine would say was:

TYPE IN PASSWORD.

A lot of help that was. He had tried everything. He had read about this kind of thing in the computer magazines he'd been devouring all week. He tried all the normal ones like *LETMEIN* and *HIITSME*. He even tried *MARTIN* and *JENNY* and Mr. Martin's first name, which was Giles. He wasn't surprised when that didn't work. He sat staring at the screen as the seconds ticked away. Tub would be getting ready to do his fainting act by now. Why on earth had they security-tagged the school computer system? Who would want to break into it?

The screen was full of failed attempts and the boring message:

TYPE IN PASSWORD.

Absentmindedly he typed it in. The screen scrolled and the most beautiful words in the English language flashed at him:

YOU ARE NOW THROUGH TO THE NETWORK.

He stared at it for a moment before realizing what he'd done. He'd followed the instructions to the letter. He'd typed in *PASSWORD*. He should have thought of that before. Mr. Martin wasn't too good on computers. He just did exactly what the machine told

him to. Mrs. Lucas must have set this up for him. Simple. He began to wonder about Mrs. Lucas. She seemed to have a weird sense of humor. From then on it was a breeze. He got through to Stick's station.

NOW? he typed.

HOLD appeared on his screen.

He held.

NOW flashed up and he was on the file server and calling up Mrs. Lucas's program.

LOAD "RAFFLE" he typed.

He saved the program and got back to Stick with *CHANGE DISK,* and settled down to work.

It looked quite simple really, though he wished he had a printout. All Mrs. Lucas seemed to have done was take the school roll for the first, second, and third years and flag some of the names. As far as he could see, the program went through the names randomly till it came up with one that was flagged, and the first one it found that had a flag on it was the winner. So the ones that were flagged had to be the ones it would select from. All he had to do was make sure the program ended up selecting him, and that meant changing the flag. Mrs. Lucas had used *F* for flag. Predictable after that password business. Well, an *F* could easily become an *E*—for enterprise, expertise, endeavor, easy. He had to change only one statement and, of course, the flag at his name on the data disk. He typed the line number.

There was a noise from the classroom and he jumped, then listened.

"Those kids. Think they make as much mess as this at home? That'll be the day."

Mr. Hughes, the janitor, was always moaning. If he caught him, George would be done for. Thank goodness he had closed the closet door. He sat there, silent and motionless, listening to Mr. Hughes saying things the kids would be reported for saying. He could hear the janitor moving around, grumbling as he went. There were several thumps as the books George had knocked over were picked up and returned to Mr. Martin's desk. George sat there, knowing the time was ticking away, hoping that Mr. Hughes wouldn't come near the closet. Mr. Hughes was saying some very interesting things about Mr. Martin's leaving his classroom unlocked. George had to admit most of it was perfectly justified and gave George a few ideas besides. It was ages before he heard the classroom door click shut and the key turn in the lock.

He turned back to the computer, leaning on the keyboard in relief. One statement to change and now he would have to hurry, thanks to Mr. Hughes. He thought of Chris Simmonds's IFS and ELSES and IF NOTS. It wasn't nearly as complicated as that. He straightened up and the line number winked at him briefly as the cursor shot over to the left-hand side of the screen. He must have leaned on the ENTER key. The line was gone. He wished again that he had a printout, but it was a simple enough statement. He retyped the line number and the statement and substituted an *E* for the *F*. Then all he had to do was flag his own name with an *E* and it was done.

He sat back, satisfied. Chris had made so much of this business. Okay, so IFS and IF NOTS could be really confusing if you didn't know what you were doing, if you weren't George Aitken, computer king.

He looked at his watch. Not much time. Kev's program should be ready to do its stuff by now. He saved the program and data to disk and got back on Stick's station.

RUN BLOWUP he instructed.

HOLD came back.

George waited for thirty seconds.

NOW? he asked.

CHAOS came the reply.

It wasn't what he was supposed to say, but it would do.

Things seemed to be going according to plan. He gave Stick instructions to switch the disk and saved the fixed program to the disk in the computer room under *RAFFLE*. It had worked like a dream. He even remembered to wipe it off Mr. Martin's disk. He checked that Mr. Hughes had in fact locked the door, and went out by the fire escape.

Easy. And if anybody even thought of George's interfering through Mr. Martin's computer— impossible, wasn't it, with Mr. Hughes there to say he'd locked the door and there had been nobody in the room.

Aitken, George
Papillon sur Mer

5

George dropped down onto the playground just as the bell rang.

"George," said a voice he recognized, "what were you doing up there?"

"Oh, hi, Sharon," said George, trying to sound casual. "How's the cello?"

Sharon played the cello—and sang in the school choir.

"What were you doing up there?" she said again. She could be really persistent sometimes.

"It was a cat," said George. "It got stuck."

"Cat?" said Sharon. "I don't see any cat."

George swallowed. It had been the first thing that came into his head. Sharon's cello always reminded him of cats for some reason. "It's gone now," he said, and began to invent a story. A few details lent an air of authenticity to any lie. "Poor little thing—stuck up there. It was terrified. Shivering. I mean, I couldn't just leave it, so I climbed up to rescue it. It wasn't easy. It struggled like mad, but I got it. It's quite safe now."

"Where?" said Sharon.

George looked around. "Must have run off. You know what cats are like—fast on their feet and not very grateful."

Sharon looked suspicious. She was much better at it than Mr. Martin.

"A cat?"

"Just a kitten really," said George. Try for sympathy this time, he thought. "Tiny little thing. Looked like a ball of fluff. You couldn't just abandon it. Somebody must have been frightening it. I think it's terrible the way people can be cruel to poor, defenseless little animals."

"Do you, George?"

George drew himself up. This was more like it.

"Of course I do," he said indignantly. "There's nothing worse than cruelty to animals."

Sharon began to soften. She had this thing about good causes like the SPCA.

"But how did it get up there in the first place if it was just a kitten?" she said, looking at the fire escape. It didn't come right down to the ground. In fact, it ended somewhere above their heads.

"It's amazing what terror can do," George said. "Or maybe it was in Mr. Martin's room. The window was open."

Sharon tutted. "Poor little thing. Are you all right? It didn't scratch you?"

George preened. Better and better. He wished he had a scratch to show her.

"Oh, no," he said. "I have this natural affinity with animals. Like a sixth sense. They trust me."

Sharon actually smiled then. "Well, I think that's marvelous, George. You must come to our next Friends of the Animals meeting. I'll let you know when it is. I didn't even know you were fond of animals."

"Oh, I am," said George. "I love them. All of them. All God's creatures and all that."

Sharon was also hot on religion. She was still smiling at him. He could have rescued a dozen cats—if there had been any to rescue. He felt like a hero. Something out of a legend—probably in shining armor. Usually with Sharon he felt like that thing they learned about in biology—an amoeba or something. He wanted to tell her he would be going to France, but maybe not—maybe it would be better to surprise her, and besides, she would ask questions if he told her now.

He was still standing there, watching Sharon drift across the playground and wondering how it was she could make the school uniform look good, when Stick and Kev hurtled around the corner.

"Where did you get that program?" Stick yelled at him. "The one you gave Kev."

George wiped off his hands. That fire escape had been dirty. Maybe he should mention it to Mr. Hughes.

"Worked okay, did it?" he said.

"That depends what you wanted it to do," said Stick. "Where did you get it?"

"Out of one of those computer mags," said George. "What happened?"

"Mrs. Lucas went mad," said Kev. "Now she won't even let me on the old PC."

"Join the club," said George. "What exactly happened?"

"Where do you want me to start?" said Stick. "With the high-pitched whine that sounded like a demented dog whistle and nearly drove you mad or the printer going crazy spewing out paper or the police siren and flashing screen?"

"Oh, good," said George. "It worked. What did Mrs. Lucas do?"

"Went bananas. What do you think?" said Stick.

"When that message came up on the screen, I thought she would blow up."

George grinned. Blowup. Mrs. Lucas wasn't the only one who could think up names.

"She liked it?"

"George, it played the first line of 'Pop Goes the Weasel' over and over and said 'Love me, I'm lonely.' Then it started with the whine again and began from scratch. The computer room is covered in paper."

"Did she try to stop it?"

"Of course she tried to stop it, but she couldn't get the printer turned off. She had to switch the whole thing off at the socket."

"Not the network," said George, "not before the disk got copied?"

Stick shook his head. "No, that was all right. You know Mrs. Lucas." He mimicked her voice: "'Switching off is an admission of defeat.' She was wild when she had to do that."

George relaxed. He'd been relying on that. Mrs. Lucas was paranoid about switching off and starting again.

"It was only four lines. You didn't tell me it would do that," Kev said.

"Neat, isn't it?" said George. "I'm proud of you, Kev. You got it exactly right."

You could see Kev wondering whether he'd

rather be on the wrong side of Mrs. Lucas or George. It was touch and go. Then he said, "Oh, right, no problem, George."

"How did Tub and Julia do?" said George.

Stick ran a hand through his hair. It was standing on end already, so it didn't make much difference.

"There was this thud," he said. "I mean, why couldn't he just lie down quietly? It wasn't as if Mrs. Lucas was supposed to see him fainting."

"I told him to do that," said Julia. "More realistic."

They hadn't noticed Tub and Julia arrive.

"I nearly did faint for real," said Tub. "'Just relax and collapse,' she said, 'it won't hurt.' So why do I have a lump on the back of my head?"

"You didn't do it right," said Julia. "If you let your whole body go limp, it doesn't hurt at all."

"How would you know?" said Tub. "You were the one who wouldn't do the fainting in the first place."

George interrupted. They could bicker for hours, given half a chance.

"The thing is, was Mrs. Lucas taken in?" he said.

Julia snorted. "Are you kidding? With Tub groaning all over the place and saying he'd gotten a concussion? Some faint!"

"What did she do?"

"Sent him off to the medical room when she finally got him on his feet, and told him not to be dramatic."

"Dramatic!" said Tub. "I've probably dislodged something in my brain."

"Something else," said Julia. Sometimes she just didn't know when to stop.

"So long as it kept her busy, it doesn't really matter," George said soothingly.

It was the wrong thing to say.

"Oh, thanks a bundle," Tub said. "Bits of my brain are floating around, bumping into other bits of my brain, and you say it doesn't matter."

"Look," said George. "The plan worked, worked like a dream. It's in the bag, folks, a sure thing. I'm coming to France."

He looked around at the faces. They didn't seem too pleased.

Some people were never happy.

George was so convinced that he was on a roll that he even had his photo taken for his ID card. Everybody who was going to France would have to have an ID card. The photo dropped out of the slot in the booth at the shopping center.

"Looks nothing like you," said Kev.

George looked at it. His hair looked black instead of sandy and his grin would have frightened the average Doberman to death.

"I don't think these machines take photographs at all," he said. "I'll bet it's a con. They just have hundreds of strips of photos in there and bang one out when you put your money in."

"You should have waited till you found out if you've gotten the ticket," said Stick. "You don't even know if you're going yet—not for sure."

George bent down and showed the photo to the dog. It began to whine and tried to climb up Stick's leg. Stick looked at it. "Does that machine do dogs?" he said.

"Of course I'm going," said George. "What could go wrong?"

"No dogs in the shopping center," said the security guard nobody had noticed yet.

"Call that a dog?" said Tub.

"Out!" said the guard.

George was still muttering about how nothing could go wrong when the security guard threw them out of the shopping center.

"When are they running the program?" said Tub.

"Monday," said George. "First thing."

"Who's doing it?" said Stick.

"Mr. Martin. Mrs. Lucas will be away taking that course."

"Mr. Martin doesn't know anything about computers," said Kev.

George grinned. "No. All he has to do is press a button. He doesn't have to know anything about computers. It's easy."

Stick fell over the dog for the fifth time and picked it up. It scrabbled up and sat on his shoulder.

"That dog thinks it's a parrot," said Tub.

"Parrots are intelligent," said Stick. "The dog doesn't qualify. You can't teach it anything. It has a lot in common with George."

"Just wait till tomorrow," said George. "Then you'll see who's learned what. I'm practically a computer expert now. You'll see."

"Pigs might fly," said Stick.

"So might dogs if I catch you," said George, lunging at him.

The dog fell off Stick's shoulder and bit him on the ankle.

"Don't you get sick of it biting you all the time?" said Tub.

Stick shrugged. "You get used to it. I've trained myself. Mind over matter. I'm impervious to pain."

"Impervious, nothing," said George. "He's started wearing two pairs of socks."

"What's *impervious* mean?" said Kev.

George looked at him. He really liked Kev. "It means things don't get through to you, Kev," he said.

"I must be it too, then," said Kev.

"What?" said Tub.

"Impervious," Kev said. "Teachers are always going on and on about how they can't get through to me, only they never told me what it was called." He seemed quite pleased.

Nobody said a thing. Not even the dog.

Nobody said anything on Monday either when Kev looked at George standing amid a sea of paper and said, "What went wrong?"

Aitken, George
Papillon sur Mer

6

Monday morning. Mr. Martin had decided that all those concerned should assemble in the school auditorium for the draw for the free ticket. He was a little nervous in case anybody should think it was fixed — understandable really, George thought.

"We have to be seen as fair, George," he said as he staggered onto the stage with the computer.

Not actually fair, George noticed, only seen as fair.

George helped him set up the computer, then wriggled his way through the crowd to where Stick, Tub, and Kev were. The hall was jammed with people.

"What happens now?" said Stick.

"Mr. Redfeather is going to say a few words, then Mr. Martin will start the program," George said.

Mr. Redfeather's few words lasted fifteen minutes and mostly concerned litter in the playground and truancy. It wasn't very often he got to speak to so many students at the same time. He pointed that out also—when he was talking about truancy. There was a very good turnout for the draw. Mr. Hughes was skulking around, reprimanding them for things they hadn't even done—yet—and moaning about the state of the classrooms and why didn't the Head mention that.

At last Mr. Redfeather got to the point. He introduced the representative from the tour company who was going to hand over the ticket, and Mr. Martin hovered by the computer, ready for the big moment. Mr. Redfeather gave him the nod and Mr. Martin coughed and shuffled a bit and pressed a few keys on the computer. Almost at once the printer began to chatter.

George held his breath. This was it.

It was a moment before he realized that something had gone wrong. It didn't take that much paper to print out one name—George Aitken. Mr. Martin glanced at the paper pouring out of the printer and went pale.

Tub scrunched something between his teeth and

the air was filled with the smell of aniseed.

"Something's up," he said.

"That's what happened with that program you gave me, George," said Kev. "Paper everywhere."

Stick grinned. "Look at Martin."

Mr. Martin was hopping around, tearing sheets of paper off and handing them to Mr. Redfeather. Mr. Redfeather was obviously trying to explain something to the guy from the tour company.

Horrible suspicions invaded George's mind. It couldn't be the program he had given Kev. For one thing, there was no police siren and flashing lights and the screen wasn't saying "Love me, I'm lonely." The screen was filled with rows and rows of names.

"More mess to clean up," Mr. Hughes said behind George's left ear. "That's all I do in this school—clean up after you kids. It was the same in that Mr. Martin's class on Friday. Piles of books all over the place and me wanting to leave early for the bowling club semifinals."

"That must have been the cat," Sharon's voice said, and George whirled around.

Sharon smiled at him. "George got it down," she said. "It was stuck on the fire escape. He thought it might have gotten into Mr. Martin's class."

"Cat?" said Mr. Hughes. "What cat? I didn't see any cat. If you've been bringing cats into school, George Aitken, I'll report you. I've told you before.

No animals. This is a school, not a zoo, though some-times you wouldn't think it, the way you kids carry on. I'll soon see about cats." He shouldered his way through the crowd toward the stage.

George looked sadly at Sharon. She was terrific, but she'd be even more terrific if she could keep her mouth shut sometimes.

"I don't think Mr. Hughes is very fond of animals," Sharon said. "I must give him a leaflet. I'll just go and explain about the cat. I don't think he understood."

George watched her as she mounted the steps to the stage and made her way through the reams of paper that covered it. Mr. Redfeather, Mr. Martin, and the guy from the tour company were huddled around the computer, and Mr. Hughes was trying to interrupt them. He saw Sharon tap him on the shoulder and start speaking. Mr. Martin shot off the stage and out of the auditorium door. Mr. Redfeather began to listen to Sharon, and George saw his eyes search the crowd.

"*George!*" he bellowed.

George's heart sank. Mr. Redfeather always called the boys by their first names when he was really mad.

"What have you done?" said Kev.

George shrugged. "I think it's the cat."

"What cat?" said Kev.

"That's just it," said George. "There wasn't one."

Kev looked puzzled. "I don't get it," he said.

"Never mind, Kev," said George. "I'm having a bit of trouble with that myself."

By the time George reached the stage, Mr. Martin was back.

"Mrs. Lucas says she can't understand it," he said.

"We'll discuss the cat in a moment, George," said Mr. Redfeather.

"What cat?" said Mr. Martin.

"The one in your classroom," said Mr. Hughes.

"What do you suggest we do?" said Mr. Redfeather.

Mr. Martin unstuck his eyes from Mr. Hughes's accusing face.

"The telephone line wasn't that good," he said. "There was a lot of background noise and she wasn't too pleased at being called away from a seminar. She talked a lot about IFS and IF NOTS and thought she might have gotten them mixed up, but she still couldn't see how this happened. You don't know anything about flags, do you?"

"Flags?" said the Head. "What have flags got to do with it?"

Mr. Martin ran a hand through his hair. "I don't know. She was in a hurry to get back to her seminar."

Mr. Martin must have phoned Mrs. Lucas.

"Did she explain how we got every single child's name out of this computer?" said Mr. Redfeather.

Mr. Martin wasn't listening. He was mouthing "What cat?" to Mr. Hughes.

"Eh?" he said to the Head.

"You haven't," said Sharon. She was standing beside the computer with sheaves of paper in her hands.

"What?" said the Head.

Sharon smiled. "You haven't gotten everybody's name. George's name isn't here, Mr. Redfeather, and as far as I can see, his is the only one missing. I don't think I'm wrong."

Sharon was never wrong. Even the Head would never have suggested that Sharon could be wrong. Sharon was on the basketball team.

"Not there?" Mr. Martin said, and the look he gave George was highly suspicious. He must have been practicing.

The Head was looking at the papers Sharon was holding. "This will have to be checked," he said. "Then I shall phone Mrs. Lucas myself, seminar or no seminar."

He stalked off the stage and the guy from the tour company said to Mr. Martin, "I've got only half an hour. I hope you get this straightened out soon."

Mr. Martin looked from Mr. Hughes to George. You could see him deciding not to say anything.

"Cup of coffee?" he said to the guy from the tour company.

It was then that Kev leaned on the front of the stage and said, "What went wrong?"

Tub and Stick stood on either side of him, saying nothing. George didn't say anything either. He knew what had gone wrong. It was all old Hughes's fault. Interrupting him like that while he was working on the program. George had got his IFS and IF NOTS mixed up after all, and instead of his name coming out, everybody else's had—everybody's but his. Not only was he not the winner. He was the only loser.

Mr. Redfeather, Mr. Martin, and the guy from the tour company were back in five minutes. Five minutes was plenty of time for George to extract the disk from the computer and put it into his inside pocket—the one where he kept his calculator. The guy from the tour company had an envelope in his hand.

"Congratulations," he said to George.

"What?" said George.

"You've won," said the guy from the tour company. "They phoned your computer teacher again. Apparently, she said she didn't know how it had happened, but if yours was the only name missing, they'd better give the ticket to you. Save a lot of trouble."

Even when the guy that was with the guy from the tour company took a photograph of the guy from the tour company handing over the ticket to him, George couldn't believe it.

Mr. Redfeather made a short announcement—a very short announcement—and suddenly George was going to France.

"I'm going to France," he said to Sharon, and Sharon smiled. He would never be an amoeba again.

"What cat?" said Mr. Martin as they got down from the stage.

Aitken, George
Papillon sur Mer

7

George was really pretty relieved when the day came to leave for France. He'd had a few sticky moments during the month since he'd gotten the ticket. First, there was Mr. Martin and the cat. By the time he'd finished inventing his story, even George was convinced there really had been a cat. It was tiring.

And, he had to admit it, it had been a mistake to produce the photo for his ID immediately. He should have waited a day or two.

"Pretty confident, George," Mr. Martin had said.

"Just optimistic," said George. "Be prepared and all that."

"I thought you got thrown out of the scouts," said Mr. Martin.

George shuffled. "I couldn't tie knots."

"How were you on flags?" said Mr. Martin. You could tell he was suspicious, only he didn't quite know what to be suspicious about.

Mrs. Lucas was worse. She handed him back his computer studies final exam.

"I've checked it, George, and the marking is right. I simply don't understand it."

George opened his mouth to say he'd never been any good at computer studies anyway, and closed it again as his eye fell on the mark circled in red at the top of the paper.

"Ninety-one percent, George," said Mrs. Lucas. "Can you explain that?"

George swallowed. Typical! You messed up a spreadsheet and you got chucked out of the class. You got a decent mark and not even a "Congratulations, George." You couldn't win. He looked at all the checks on the paper. He'd never seen so many checks all together on one page. It must have been that boning up on computer hacking he'd done. Who said crime didn't pay?

"I worked really hard, Mrs. Lucas," he said in perfect truth.

Mrs. Lucas looked at him over her glasses. "But at what, George, at what?" she said. "I see you were particularly good on how to take care of disks."

"Oh, thanks," said George.

This was better.

"So how did you manage to wipe the disk with the ticket selection program on it?"

It wasn't better after all.

"I took it only for safekeeping," said George. "It was just unlucky my calculator was switched on."

"And wiped the disk," said Mrs. Lucas.

George didn't say anything. He couldn't have Mrs. Lucas coming back and examining the program.

Mrs. Lucas sighed. "Enjoy France, George," she said. "One way or another, you probably deserve it."

Then there was Sharon and her Friends of the Animals meetings. Definitely not George's scene, but he could make sacrifices. He even wore the badge. He was wearing it when he turned up to catch the bus that was to take them to Portsmouth to catch the ferry.

"Why are you wearing a badge with a pig on it?" said Kev.

"It isn't a pig," said George, looking down at it, "is it?" Upside down it could have been anything.

"Looks like a pig to me," said Kev.

Sharon sauntered up, dressed in summer pastels. "It's a Friends of the Animals badge, Kevin," she said. "We all wear one."

"Yours isn't a pig," said Kev.

Sharon fingered her butterfly badge. "I thought this suited me," she said.

Julia appeared at Kev's elbow. "So why did you pick a pig, George?" she said. "Think it suited you?"

"Sharon gave it to me," said George, still squinting down at the badge. He looked up. Julia was grinning.

"It's a very rare pig," said Sharon. "An Andalusian hunchback. It's an endangered species."

Julia snorted. Ah, well, thought George, it's better than an amoeba. He wondered if they made badges of amoebas. He wondered if anybody knew what an amoeba looked like. On the genetic scale you could do worse than a pig—he told himself. Julia was still snorting and grunting.

"Where's Stick?" George said to shut her up.

"He had to take the dog for a walk," said Julia. "He was only half packed when I left."

"He'll have to hurry up," said Sharon. "Here comes the bus. Why didn't he pack last night?"

"He did," said Julia. "At least, Mom did it for him, but he unpacked it all again after she'd gone to work this morning. He was looking for a T-shirt he wanted to wear."

"Did he find it?" said Kev.

"Under his bed," said Julia, "only by that time his stuff was all over the place and the dog had to go out."

"You could have taken the dog," said George.

"The dog won't come with me," said Julia. "It likes Stick."

"It bites him," said George.

"Sign of affection," Julia said.

"Tub's on the bus," said Kev, which at least put a stop to hostilities between George and Julia.

The bus drew up, and Mr. Martin began rounding them up to put their luggage in the back. Jenny, Kev's social worker, was checking off names on her list at the front of the bus.

"Looking forward to the trip, Kev?" she said as she checked his name off.

Kev settled down for a chat. George shoved past him and went to the back of the bus.

"How come you're on the bus already?" he said to Tub.

Tub grinned. "Driver lives next door. Saved my walking."

George threw himself down on the seat beside him. "Talk about lazy."

"At least I grabbed the backseat," said Tub.

"Stick isn't here yet," said George.

Kev came lumbering up the aisle, followed by Julia. Sharon sat down at the front beside the door and the rest of the bus filled up. Jenny checked her list again. Everybody seemed to be there except Stick. Mr. Martin looked at his watch, and Mr. Bell, the English teacher, started moaning about being kept waiting and how he hadn't even wanted to come in the first place. Nobody liked Mr. Bell. He was the sarcastic type. George wondered what the headmaster had on him—from the blackmail point of view.

Fifteen minutes passed. Twenty minutes. Candy wrappers flew around the bus and cans of juice sprayed. One of the freshmen had to get off and be sick—and they hadn't even started yet. The bus driver started revving the engine. Mr. Bell was telling the entire bus about traffic jams he had been in. Mr. Martin was trying to persuade another freshman that he didn't really want to go to the bathroom. Jenny was smiling and saying it wasn't far to Portsmouth and she thought Stick would turn up any minute, when around the corner appeared a vision.

It was tall and skinny and its arms and legs were going in all directions at the same time. A suitcase hung from one hand and bumped against its legs. Bits of clothes were bursting out of the sides and only one lock was fastened. It was wearing a grubby yellow T-shirt, and over its shoulder was a sports bag that seemed to be gyrating out of time with everything else. It was Stick.

The entire bus cheered, all except Mr. Bell. He was saying how nice it was of Stick to honor us with his presence. The bus was on the move almost before Stick was on it. He came swaying up the aisle, butting people on the head with his sports bag.

"Mom would go mad if she knew you were wearing that dirty T-shirt," Julia said.

"Mom won't see it, will she?" said Stick.

"And it's too small for you."

"I like it. It's meant to be tight."

"Where have you been?" said George.

Stick collapsed on the backseat. "Bit of trouble with the packing," he said, stowing his sports bag under the seat.

"What's that noise?" said Tub.

"Which one?" said Julia. The freshmen had started to sing.

"Sort of rumbling noise," said Tub, "coming from under the seat."

"It's the engine," said Stick, "what do you think?"

George had something else on his mind. "Why don't you go and sit with the freshmen, Julia?"

You had to be diplomatic, he thought, you couldn't just tell her to shove off.

"I'm with you," Julia said.

Diplomacy. Patience.

"I know that," he said. "That's why I'm asking you why you don't go and sit with the freshmen."

Maybe she hadn't understood the first time. Julia looked at him, and he didn't like what he saw.

"Remember you asked me to find out about Mrs. Lucas's program?" she said.

"Yeah."

"And I did."

"Yeah."

"And you said, was it okay?"

"Yeah."

"And I said, yes . . ."

"Yeah."

". . . for the moment."

George was visited by a terrible suspicion. He'd known at the time it was too good to be true.

"So?" he said.

"So I'm with you," said Julia, looking around them.

"For the entire trip?" said Stick.

Julia grinned. "Every minute."

"But that's blackmail," said Tub.

"Isn't it?" said Julia.

Kev was struggling. "You mean you'll tell about the program if we don't let you hang out with us?"

Julia nodded. "Got it in one, Kev."

"My mom says blackmail's a disgrace," said Tub.

Julia gave him a look. "The Head does it. Ask Mr. Martin," she said.

George lay back in his seat, defeated. And to think he'd been looking forward to this trip. What was it Mrs. Lucas had said? "One way or another you probably deserve it."

Aitken, George
Papillon sur Mer

8

George came out of his nightmare vision of Julia's tagging along with them for the whole vacation to hear Stick saying to Tub, "It's your imagination, or more likely your stomach rumbling, the amount of garbage you eat."

Tub was indignant. "You should talk. That's your third bar of chocolate."

"I'm growing," said Stick. "I can't do without food, can I?"

"You've never tried," said Tub.

"He's right," said Kev.

Stick turned on him. "Don't you start. Three measly chocolate bars. You'd think it was an orgy."

Mr. Bell's voice came over the loudspeaker system, telling them they were just entering the Portsmouth ferry port. He'd hardly been off it since he found out how it worked.

"No, I mean about the rumbling," said Kev. "Tub's right."

Tub leaned back, satisfied.

"Told you so," he said, and took a paper bag out of his pocket. "Have an aniseed ball, Kev."

Several things happened at once. Kev took a candy and crunched it, releasing the smell of aniseed all over them. Mr. Bell said, "Just sit in your places till the bus stops." The freshmen started to cheer, and Stick's sports bag shot out from under the seat and began to growl.

George was on it before Stick could move. "You brought it," he said. "Trouble with packing? No wonder you had trouble with packing. What did you do to it? Sedate it?"

Stick grabbed the bag, but George hung on. The bag began to whine.

"You'll squash it," said Stick.

"I'll squash you," said George. "How stupid can you get?"

"Starting at the front in an orderly fashion," Mr. Bell's voice said before it was drowned in the uproar as the entire bus rushed for the door—all except the backseat. The bus lurched to a stop and the sports bag thudded to the floor and howled.

"No shouting," yelled Mr. Bell.

Kev picked up the bag and unzipped it. The dog leapt out and clung to him, licking his face. Kev seemed pleased.

"It never liked me much before," he said.

"It's the aniseed," Tub said. "Dogs love aniseed."

A mangled necktie dangled from the dog's left ear.

"Did you think putting it in a school uniform would help?" said George.

"It's a muzzle," said Stick. "Best I could do. It must have gotten it off."

George ducked down and thrust the dog back into the bag. It yelped, but everyone else was too busy climbing over one another to get off the bus to notice.

"Mr. Martin will go crazy," said George. "You can't take it, Stick."

Stick looked pained. "Six months quarantine," he said. "Six months without the dog. You don't know what it's like, George."

"And what happens when Mom finds out?" said Julia.

Stick shrugged. "She'll get over it."

"What's she going to say when she gets home and finds no dog?" said Tub, and dropped some aniseed balls into the bag. The bag began to dance across the floor of the bus. Stick picked it up.

"I thought of that," he said. "I left her a note."

"Off the bus, you at the back." Mr. Bell's head was thrust around the front seat. "Unless you relish spending your vacation on the bus."

"Coming, sir," said George.

"A note?" said Julia as they made their way down the aisle.

"I thought she might worry about it," said Stick.

Julia shook her head. "She'll kill you," she said.

She said it again as they got off the bus and saw her mom standing there talking to Mr. Martin, only she added the word *slowly*.

Mr. Martin was looking bewildered. He turned as Stick got down from the bus, but Stick's mom was quicker. She was halfway across to them before Mr. Martin could get a word out. Stick got behind Kev for protection.

"What are you doing here, Mom? Come to see us off?"

"See you off is just about right," his mom said. "If I hadn't had to come back for some files I'd forgotten, I'd have been too late to stop you. As it is I nearly broke my neck getting here before the bus did. Where is it?"

She and Stick were playing Here We Go 'Round the Mulberry Bush with Kev as the bush.

"I left you a note, Mom."

"A note! I read the note." Her voice was rising. A small crowd began to gather around. "You took the dog and left a note." She was really yelling now.

"I thought you might worry," said Stick. "I thought you might think it had been kidnapped."

"*Kidnapped!*" she screeched. Mr. Bell's loudspeaker system had nothing on her.

George stood on the sidelines, watching. Stick and his mom were still circling Kev. Kev kept trying to get out of the way. The crowd was getting bigger.

"Kidnapped!" yelled Stick's mom again. She seemed to be struck by the idea. "What do you think it is—a racehorse?"

"It's a pedigree," said Stick.

"I'm being kidnapped," said a small, stout child to George.

She was wearing jeans and a tour T-shirt and was sucking a lollipop. Her T-shirt seemed to be spattered with mud. It looked worse than Stick's. She came up to his waist.

"Oh, yeah," said George. "I like your T-shirt."

"I don't," said the small, stout child. "I'm going to wear nice clothes when I'm kidnapped."

There was some action on the Stick/Kev/Mom front.

"She's right, you know," Kev said to Stick.

"What?" said Stick.

"Your mom. She's right. It isn't a racehorse. It isn't even a greyhound."

Stick stopped circling Kev so that he could argue with him.

"It's my dad's," the small kid beside George was saying.

George looked down. She was pointing at her T-shirt.

"Your dad must be pretty small," he said.

She sucked on her lollipop thoughtfully. "Mom says he used to be really big."

George's attention was distracted by a yell from Stick. His mom had caught him. It had been a tactical error—stopping.

"Oh, yeah?" George said to the kid. "What happened to him, your dad? Stick's mom get hold of him?"

Kev sauntered across just as a big guy in a leather jacket appeared.

"Tamarind," the guy said to the kid. "I told you not to wander off," and he grabbed her.

George spared them a look as they walked off across the car park. What an imagination.

"It's a tree," said Kev.

"What is?" said George.

"A tamarind," said Kev. "It's a tree."

Kev knew the strangest things, mostly about trees and plants and stuff like that.

"What do you give for Stick's chances?" George said.

The crowd was close to them now, but you could still hear Stick's mom.

Kev grinned. "Mr. Martin sent Jenny to straighten it out."

George shook his head. "She'll have a job."

"She straightens my dad out," said Kev. "All the time. Just talks to him. She's great at that."

"George!" said a voice, and George snapped to attention.

"Oh, hi, Sharon."

"What's going on? Why is Paul's mother here?"

George looked into Sharon's blue eyes and tried for sincerity.

"Just came to see him off," he said. "What with Julia going as well, she's going to miss them."

Sharon frowned. "There seems to be some trouble about the dog."

George worked on the sincerity. "She brought it down to say good-bye. Stick's very fond of it."

Sharon relaxed.

"Oh, I didn't know that," she said. "I must tell him about our Friends of the Animals society. I'll get him a badge. I always carry some with me."

George smiled. "Make it a chicken," he said as she bustled off.

And get one for me, he nearly added as he saw Mr. Martin bearing down on him.

"Aitken!"

Unlike the Head, Mr. Martin used last names when he was mad.

"Nothing to do with me," said George.

"It is from now on," said Mr. Martin.

"What do you mean?" said George. "I tried to tell him. . . ."

"So you did know."

Stupid.

"I forgot. I had other things on my mind."

"Like getting on the trip."

Deeper and deeper.

"Look, Mr. Martin—" He didn't get a chance to finish.

"All I'm saying is, if I get any more trouble from one of your mob, you'll be the one I'll blame."

"But that isn't fair," said George.

"Fair or not, that's the way it is, George. Talking to any of the rest is like spitting into the wind. I hold you personally responsible for anything that bunch does."

"Mr. Martin . . ." George tried to appeal.

"Unless you want to deal with Mr. Bell."

George collapsed.

"Okay, you win."

Mr. Martin laughed. It sounded just a little wild. "You think so? I've got Mr. Bell to deal with."

"Where is he anyway?" said George.

"Gone to check departure time," said Mr. Martin,

and he seemed as relieved as George felt.

"At least you've got Jenny," said George, thinking of Stick's mom.

Mr. Martin brightened up. "That's it," he said.

"What?" said George.

"I'll get hold of Sharon. She can help you keep them in line if anybody can."

George watched him striding away. Sharon. Somehow he didn't think that was going to go down too well. He found himself wondering if Stick's mom would give him a lift home. Even the dog's company seemed attractive at the moment.

Mr. Bell came back and rounded them up. As they all loped off toward the ferry, they could still hear Stick's mom's voice, even above the barking of the dog.

"Why is all your stuff falling out of your suitcase, and why are you wearing that filthy T-shirt?"

"Told you she wouldn't like it," said Julia.

"Oh, shut up," said Stick.

No, thought George, a lift home with Stick's mom wouldn't be a good idea. He'd go on the trip. At least he'd get peace to be miserable.

9

The ferry trip was fairly uneventful, mainly because Sharon was doing her prison-guard routine. Sharon was good at the prison-guard bit. Besides which, the rest of them were crushed. Stick's mom did that to you. Even Julia was pretty silent, and she hadn't been on the wrong side of the shouting. Stick was the worst though. He was really down.

"The dog would just have been a pest," said George. "It was a crazy idea."

Stick shook his head. "Six months," he said. "And a lecture as well."

"It would have been worse if you'd actually taken

the dog," said George, "when you came back, I mean."

"You think it could have been worse?"

George thought for a moment, looking for something comforting to say. Stick was right. It couldn't have been worse, just . . .

"It could have gone on longer," he said. "When you got back. At least we had a boat to catch."

"Yeah," said Stick, "maybe you're right."

It was something. George looked around him. The small, stout child was over by the rail, eating an ice-cream cone. She was wearing a tiny biker's jacket over her T-shirt. Maybe that was her dad's as well.

"That kid says she's being kidnapped," said George to take Stick's mind off his own problems.

"Don't talk to me about kidnapping," said Stick.

A shadow fell across them. It was Sharon.

"I didn't realize you were so fond of your little dog, Paul," she said. "I've brought you a Friends of the Animals badge."

She bent down and pinned it on his dirty T-shirt, then carefully wiped her hands on her hanky. Sharon always had a hanky. George tried not to look at the badge.

"What is it?" said Stick, peering down at it.

"A giraffe," said Sharon.

Stick unfolded himself and stood up. His legs seemed to go on and on forever.

"Oh, very funny," he said, and bounced off.

"What's wrong with him?" said Sharon.

"He's sensitive about his height," said George.

Sharon looked puzzled, then shrugged her shoulders. "You'd better come and help me, George," she said. "The freshmen are changing their money into francs."

"What's wrong with that?" said George.

Sharon gave him one of her laser looks. "Julia is trying to work something out with the man behind the desk."

By the time they got there, Tub was having a conversation in broken English with the man in charge of changing money. They seemed to be talking about Tub's mom and Adam Smith, which was okay. What was odd was that Tub was the one speaking broken English. The French guy's English was quite good. George waded in and yanked Tub out.

"Where's Julia?"

Tub pointed.

Julia was in the middle of a crowd of freshmen, distributing francs and arguing. She seemed to be charging them a fee.

"It was my idea to change all our money together," she said when George grabbed her. "That way they charged only one commission."

It took a while to get that straightened out, and the whole business left George feeling a bit weak, so in a quiet moment he wedged himself out of sight behind a pile of life rafts and let the world go on without him for a while. Admittedly, he missed a little excitement, like Tub's first encounter with real French pastries and Kev's instant addiction to the slot machines that only Jenny's influence tore him away from, but he couldn't honestly say he minded. By the time the ferry docked and they piled into the waiting bus, they were all too tired to care where they were going. As they crawled through customs, the driver dimmed the lights and everybody pulled down the little window shades. George's eyes closed.

He was jolted awake by the bus braking suddenly. The window shade next to him shot up. It was pitch dark outside. They seemed to be in the middle of nowhere. George peered out. He was just about level with a parking lot, hedged on the side nearest the road. Being high up, he could see over the hedge. There were two cars in the lot, and George saw a man in a leather jacket get out of one, look around, and then open the back door. The inside light went on and George saw the man reach up. The light went off but not before George had seen the kid in the micro biker's jacket lying bundled up in a blanket on the backseat, fast asleep. No wonder, if she was as tired as George was. His eyes were closing again. He thought he saw the man in the leather jacket lift her out of the car and transfer her to the other one, a big black one with smoked windows so dark you couldn't see through them. So dark . . . so dark . . . George was asleep.

The next time he woke up the bus had stopped and Mr. Bell was shaking his shoulder.

"Wake up," said Mr. Bell. "Time to go to bed."

Even George, half asleep as he was, didn't think that sounded quite right. They shuffled out of the bus and grabbed their luggage from the pile outside a long, low building.

"What's that funny smell?" said Tub.

"Stick's T-shirt," said Julia.

"No, it isn't," said Stick, but you could see he was too tired to make much of it.

SUNSHINE BUS COMP

"Fresh air," said Mr. Martin. "And the sea. You can hear it."

"What? That roaring," said Kev through an enormous yawn. "I thought that was just me."

"Not this time, Kev," said Mr. Martin. "Even you can't compete with the Côte Sauvage."

"The what?" said Julia. She was yawning now as well.

"The wild coast," Sharon's voice said.

George was thinking that you didn't throw out challenges like that to Kev and get away with it. Mr. Martin should have known better. Then he was in a room with bunk beds for four. He had just enough energy left to beat Kev to the top bunk. Self-preservation at work again. He didn't even feel his head hit the pillow, he was asleep so fast.

He was awakened in the morning by a bell in the distance and a lot of crashing around nearby.

"What's up?" he said. "Has there been a fire?"

Kev loomed over him despite the fact that he was in the top bunk. "I've been outside already," he said.

"Why didn't you stay there?" said George. "There's more room for you out there. You woke me up."

"It's time to get up anyway," said Kev. "That's what the bell's for."

George was fully awake now. So were Tub and Stick. They all looked at Kev. His eyes were shining and his grin was so broad, he looked as if he'd swallowed a banana sideways.

"What's up with you?" said Stick.

"Nothing," said Kev. "I told you. I've been outside."

"Big deal," said Stick.

"What's for breakfast?" said Tub.

George was still concentrating on Kev. "What's it like out there, Kev?" he said.

Kev's grin got even wider. "Wonderful," he said. "Absolutely wonderful."

And it was.

Aitken, George
Papillon sur Mer

10

The dormitory cabins were built around a large square with a dining hall and game room at one side. That wasn't what was so impressive, though. What was so impressive was the beach you could see from the dining hall windows. Miles of it and the sea curling over it in white-crested waves.

"Surfing," said Kev, "and canoeing and sailing. There's a shed down there on the beach full of boats and things."

George opened his mouth to say that the average tidal wave would have its work cut out supporting Kev on a surfboard, but closed it again. Kev was looking particularly massive in an OP T-shirt and Bermuda shorts. The Bermuda shorts gave a new meaning to the word *colorful* and he didn't want to spoil things for him.

"What's the plan, then?" he said instead.

"They put up lists each day," Stick said. "You get to try everything and then you choose what you want to concentrate on."

"How do you know?" said Tub, or at least that's what it sounded like. He was concentrating on breakfast.

"Julia told me," said Stick.

Julia appeared at their table on cue.

"We have canoeing this morning," she said.

"What do you mean *we?*" said Tub without much hope.

"The lists are up," said Julia. "I got Jenny to put me with you. I'm feeling homesick."

"You only just got here," said Stick. "How can you be feeling homesick?"

"I'll feel better if I'm with you, Stick," she said, and smiled.

George looked accusingly at Kev. "Your social worker's too soft," he said.

Kev grinned. "I know."

After breakfast they were issued ID cards with their names and the address of the camp on them. The teachers supervised them while they slotted their photos into the plastic pocket on the card. Then the camp director went on for ten minutes about water safety. His English was really good and he didn't look like the type you would want to get on the wrong side of. After that they walked down to the beach to get their canoes. The schedule was really arranged well. They were to have an activity in the morning according to a rota so that everybody got a turn at everything. In the afternoon they could choose their activity on a first-come-first-served basis or go into the village or join one of the organized groups for an outing to places of interest. Tub wasn't impressed by the "places of interest" bit.

"I know what that will be," he said while they were waiting for their canoes, "old ruins and things."

"That's the educational element, Tub," Jenny said. Jenny was in charge of issuing the canoes.

"Your dad would be pleased," said Julia.

"My dad isn't the one who has to trail around ruins," said Tub. "I think I'll go and look at the village this afternoon."

"It isn't just old buildings," said Jenny. "There are lots of other things to see as well."

"What sort of things?" Stick said.

"Standing stones, for instance," said Jenny. "Some of the most famous standing stones in the world are in Brittany."

"What do you mean standing stones?" said Tub.

"Stones don't do anything else. I mean, they don't move around much, do they?"

"No, Tub," said Jenny, "but these are special stones. Some people think they were erected by the druids. Others think they belonged to even more ancient civilizations. Nobody is quite sure, but they seem to be something to do with religious rites."

"See what I mean," said Tub. "Churches."

"Stonehenge," said George.

Jenny smiled. "That's right, George."

"I thought that had to do with hippies and midsummer and telling the time from the stars," said Stick.

"Well . . ." said Jenny, then, "This one will do for you, Kev," and she hauled out an enormous canoe.

"Menhirs," said Kev.

"Same to you," said Stick.

"That's what they're called, those standing stones," Kev said. "Menhirs."

"Kev's quite right," said Jenny.

Stick prodded Kev. "How come you know that?"

Kev grabbed his canoe and hefted it onto his back. "*Asterix*," he said. "I really like *Asterix*," and he began to trudge away down the beach.

"Hey, Kev," shouted Julia. "Who's your favorite character in the Asterix books?"

Kev turned, balancing the canoe on his back. It stuck up in the air over his head.

"Obelix," he said.

They all laughed, and Jenny gave out the rest of the canoes.

"And no fooling around," she said.

"Who, us?" said George.

In fact, the canoeing was quite a success. They had all done it before, in the local swimming pool, so they knew the basics, and the instructor kept them with him throughout the lesson, like a duck with ducklings. Even Julia wasn't that much bother. Of course, it helped that they all had their own canoes. It saved a lot of fighting.

They had lunch in camp and nobody argued much with Tub's idea of going into the village. They were all quite eager to see it, but they let Tub think they were doing him a favor.

The village was bigger than they had expected—more of a small town really.

Tub immediately headed for one of the cafés in the square.

"You've just had lunch," said Julia.

"Mr. Martin was telling me about these pancakes," said Tub. "It's a kind of national dish in Brittany. You know what my dad said—it's educational."

"Pancakes?" said George. "First I've heard of pancakes being educational."

"I couldn't eat a thing," said Julia.

Stick was muttering, "Educational pancakes. Sounds okay to me."

George, Julia, and Kev left Stick and Tub to the pancakes and set off to explore the village. It didn't take that long. There was a small fair that wasn't open yet, a row of cafés along the sea front, and some shops that seemed still closed for lunch.

"Definitely Tub's kind of place," said George.

"What are those?" said Julia.

George looked across the street. There was a courtyard with what looked like open iron-framed carriages parked in it. They had solid rubber wheels and a steering wheel and a sort of canopy on top. They seemed to be pedal powered. There was a sign on the gate of the courtyard. ROSALIES, it said.

"Whatever they are, they belong to Rosalie," said George. "Let's go and ask."

There was an old woman in a little hut at the back of the courtyard, and it took them a while to figure out the fact that she wasn't Rosalie. Rosalies were what the carriages were called, and they were for rent. They let Julia handle the money angle. She seemed to have a great deal of knowledge about that side of things. They had to hand over their IDs and the old woman pointed them toward a Rosalie with three seats.

"Why does she want ID?" said Kev.

"In case we run away with her Rosalie, I suppose," George said.

Kev looked at it. "You wouldn't get far in that," he said.

There was a reasonable-size seat above each of the two sets of wheels and a smaller one squashed in between. George looked at Julia. "I want to pedal," she said. "The middle seat hasn't got any pedals."

"You're the smallest," said George.

Julia stuck to her guns.

"Look," said George, "we've got the thing for only an hour. Tell you what, I pedal first half, you pedal second."

"What about Kev?" said Julia.

George looked at the middle seat.

"Can you imagine Kev getting into that?" he said.

George took the steering wheel and Julia sulked in the middle seat. Kev concentrated on the pedals and so did George, after a moment. With so much power on one side, he had to work hard to stop them going around in circles. It was a marvelous way to see the place. Once they got the hang of it, they were even cornering on all four wheels. Admittedly, it took them a while to realize they should be driving on the other side of the road, but there wasn't all that much traffic and the brakes seemed to work quite well. If Kev had one fault, it was not knowing his own strength, and if he had another one, it was looking everywhere but where he was going. As he pointed out, George was steering.

It was when they came to a traffic circle that George began to see the flaw in this argument. He slowed down, trying to decide which way to go. Kev just kept on pedaling and the Rosalie began to go in a circle. At that moment a large black car came around the circle. George had just enough time to wonder what it reminded him of and to realize that they were going the wrong way, and then the car was bearing down on them.

"Stop!" yelled George, mostly to the car.

Kev stopped pedaling, and the Rosalie began to turn the other way, right into the path of the car.

"Not you," George shouted. "Pedal."

Kev pedaled. The Rosalie shot across the traffic circle just as the car passed, grazing their back bumper as it went. There was a tinkle of broken glass on the road.

"He's smashed our lights," said Julia.

"Better than smashing us," said George.

He was concentrating on steering the Rosalie toward a narrow side street and pedaling hard enough to match Kev. They shot into the narrow opening and out again almost immediately and into the village square. A quick glance caught Tub's and Stick's faces as they rattled past the café. Tub had a forkful of pancake halfway to his mouth. Julia waved as they clattered through the square.

"Slow down," yelled George.

Kev stopped pedaling, Julia slammed on the brakes on Kev's side, and the Rosalie slewed around in a circle and shot Julia forward. She grabbed for the canopy and there was a tearing sound. The Rosalie came to rest in front of the café.

"What are those things?" said Tub. "One of them passed by earlier."

"Rosalies," said Julia as she untangled herself from the ripped fringe of the canopy. "What did you want to do that for, George?"

"It was you who slammed on the brake," said George.

"You said to stop," said Julia.

"I said to slow down," said George. "Now look what you've done." He held up the tattered remnants of the fringe.

"Rosalie isn't going to be very pleased," said Stick.

George groaned and Kev launched into an explanation.

"Do they all have names?" said Tub.

"No," said Kev, "they're all called Rosalie."

"No imagination, the French," said Tub, "but they make great pancakes."

George had assessed the damage. "I might have some pancakes after all," he said. "It's your turn to pedal anyway, Julia. You can take it back if you like."

Julia gave him a look. A bit of practice and she'd

be nearly as good as Sharon. George wondered how girls did it. Maybe they were born with a talent for laser looks.

"No deal," said Julia as if he hadn't gotten the message.

In the end the five of them took it back. Unfortunately, the village seemed to have decided that lunchtime was over. Stick and Kev did the pedaling, and the rest hung on to the Rosalie wherever they could. Quite a number of people stopped what they were doing to watch them.

The bickering reached its peak just outside the courtyard. Nobody wanted to go in.

"Just leave it here," said Tub.

"In the street? Somebody might steal it," said George.

"You should be so lucky," said Stick.

In the end they got behind it and gave it a gentle shove through the gate of the courtyard. They heard a grinding sound as it connected with several other Rosalies, and made a run for it.

They were glad when they got back to camp.

"Mission accomplished," said George.

"We should be in the commandos," said Tub.

"You won't be able to rent one again," said Stick.

"I didn't even have a turn at pedaling," said Julia.

"I wouldn't mind taking one out again," said Kev.

"The camp director has had a phone call," said a voice.

They looked up. Nobody had noticed Mr. Bell.

"What?" said George.

"The camp director," said Mr. Bell. "He's had a call from the woman who rents out the Rosalies."

They were too stunned to protest.

"How did she know where to find us?" said George.

Mr. Bell gave him a look. "You trying to be funny, boy?"

"Never felt less like it," said George.

"Must be lack of brains, then," said Mr. Bell. "If you don't use your brain, it curls up and dies—if you had one in the first place, that is."

They didn't say anything. The best way to deal with Mr. Bell was to say as little as possible.

"You left your IDs when you rented the Rosalie, didn't you?"

George felt really stupid. He'd forgotten.

"The camp director's office—now!" said Mr. Bell. "And the Rosalies are out of bounds. If I had my way, the whole village would be out of bounds."

"Do you think he means us as well?" said Stick as Mr. Bell strode off.

George looked at Tub and Stick.

"It was nothing to do with you," he said. "You weren't even there. You were eating pancakes peacefully till we came along."

Tub and Stick exchanged a look.

"We'll come anyway," said Tub. "Anything for a laugh. Right, Stick?"

Stick shrugged. "I'm not doing anything else. It'll pass the time."

George looked at Tub and Stick. They were mostly useless, but you couldn't deny it—they had their moments.

"Do you think they'll use truth drugs?" said George.

"He said camp *director* not camp *commandant*," said Stick.

"We could always make a break for it," said Tub. "Like that film they always put on TV at Christmas with the guy jumping the wire on a motorcycle. You know, the one about the prisoner-of-war camp. My mom watches it every year."

"I know that one," said Kev. "That's the one with the guy who keeps being flung in the slammer."

"Same guy," said Tub.

"Motorcycles. Rosalies. Same thing really," said George.

"There was a tune they used to whistle," said Julia.

"So there was," said Stick, and began to whistle as they tramped across the compound. They all joined in.

Aitken, George
Papillon sur Mer

■■

It was the next morning at breakfast. George was trying to forget the scene in the camp director's office and it wasn't easy, even after a night's sleep. That guy spoke really good English, and the way he used it, *camp commandant* was nearer the mark than *camp director*.

"Each sailing instructor takes six at a time," Julia was saying. "Sharon's the other one in our group."

The others started to yell at her.

"It isn't my fault," Julia said. "Mr. Martin did it. He's put Sharon with us as a watchdog."

"George," said Tub, "did you hear that? What are you going to do about it?"

"Eh?" said George. "What's the problem?"

They tried to tell him, but he wasn't listening. Julia's words had sunk in, and the scene in the camp director's office was a million years ago. He was seeing himself skimming over the waves, eyes narrowed against the glare of the sea. Aitken was at the helm. Sharon was saying "aye, aye, sir" or "my hero" or something like that.

It didn't quite work out like that, but even when Mr. Martin got them in a corner afterward and grilled them about the incident, Tub maintained that they'd saved the instructor's life. Not that he was grateful; at least, he hadn't sounded grateful. Of course, that might have been just the French way of showing gratitude; after all, he was speaking French at the time. Well, not speaking exactly, yelling French and not slowly either the way you're supposed to do with foreigners. Still, everybody knew the French were very excitable.

The first thing the instructor did was issue them with life jackets and show them a boat, as if they couldn't recognize a boat when they saw one. He even said it—"This is a boat." Actually it was more like "Zees ees eh boot," but it was no problem, not if you were used to Tub talking with his mouth full, which was most of the time. What was surprising was Kev.

"Batto," he said.

They all looked at him.

"What?" said Julia.

"Batto," said Kev again.

"Oh, yeah," said Stick.

"It's French for boat. *Bateau*," said Sharon.

They all looked at Kev in wonder. He had trouble with English.

"How do you know that?" said George.

Kev shrugged. "It just came to me," he said.

Impressive. The instructor was impressed as well. He said a few words in French to Kev. Kev just smiled, then the instructor was at it again.

They got "zees ees eh roop," "zees ees eh seel," and even "zees ees eh noor," which took them a minute to figure out even though they were looking at it. Then it was down to the nitty-gritty. There was an arrangement of tires enclosing a small bay where they were to "praktees hundling ze boot." Sharon had sailed before, naturally, so she was able to translate the English if not the French. Things like the "raw dare"—the thing you steer with. The French was no problem. They just ignored it.

After about half an hour explaining things in funny English, the instructor put them into boats. He went in one with Kev and Tub and put Sharon in charge of Stick, George, and Julia.

"Just because she keeps saying things like 'going about' and knows what tacking is," said Julia, disgusted. "Showing off, that's all it is."

"At least she knows what she's talking about," said George. "She's got certificates for sailing."

Stick was looking around the beach. "This place is like that page out of our first-year-French book," he said. The one with the picture of all those people on the beach. What was it called? 'Soor la plaj.' "

George looked around. He was right. The beach was crammed with kids. Kids in boats. Kids in canoes. Kids on windsurfing boards, or off windsurfing boards mostly. Sharon climbed into the boat beside them.

"We're going to capsize," she said.

"Too many people in the boat," said Julia. "Three's enough."

"On purpose," said Sharon. "It's the first thing you learn."

"Can't see capsizing being any problem," said Stick. He was looking at the other boat. Kev was wedged in at one end. The other end was sticking out of the water.

"Pay attention," said Sharon.

They paid attention. There was a lecture coming.

"Capsize drill," said Sharon. "I shall stand on the edge of the boat, take hold of the boom, and pull the boat over. *You*," she emphasized the word, "you will float inside the boat. I shall then swim around to the sailboard—"

"What's that?" said Stick.

"The piece sticking out of the bottom into the water," said George.

Stick looked down. "This?" he said, waggling a slice of wood.

The boat rocked.

"Don't do that," said Sharon, and continued with the lecture. "I shall stand on the sailboard, take a jib sheet, and pull up, thus righting the boat."

"Did she say *thus*?" said Stick.

"Do you know what she's talking about?" muttered Julia to George.

George tried to look knowledgeable. "No," he said.

"Any questions?" said Sharon.

"When do we do the mutiny drill?" said Julia.

Sharon ignored her. "Remember, stay inside the boat. I shall need you to pull me back in. Ready?"

"Okay," said Stick.

"Is there any choice?" said Julia.

"Aye, aye, sir," said George. You had to be professional about these things.

He admired the way she balanced on the side of the boat. He admired the way she hauled on the boom, the metal pole that the bottom of the sail was attached to. He didn't even mind when she pulled the boat over and landed them all in the water. He just floated there, hanging on to the boat. And when she suddenly emerged on the other side and stood poised on the sailboard and hauled on a rope and the boat began to right itself, he felt quite poetic. It was a pity he didn't leave it at that, but he didn't. He scrambled up the side of the boat, hoisting himself up on the rim. It was a mistake. When the boom came over, it caught him smack between the shoulder blades. He grabbed for something, anything, and found a rope, one of the jib sheets, and suddenly he'd done it all by himself. He'd made the boat capsize. He emerged spluttering beside her in the water.

"How's that?" he said. "I'm a quick learner."

Sharon gave him one of her laser looks.

By the time they had all gotten into the boat at the same time, they'd had a lot of practice in capsizing. An immersion course, you could say, thought George. Like Chris Simmonds's computer course. They bailed out the boat a bit and looked across at the other one. It wasn't there. At least, it wasn't all there. There were chunks of it floating around, but none of the pieces amounted to what you would call a boat.

Something that might have been a whale, except that it was too colorful, grabbed the side of the boat and they rocked dangerously.

"What's French for 'help,' George?" said Kev.

"Why?" said George. "Are you thinking of drowning us? Get off the boat."

"I think it's what that French guy's shouting," said Kev.

They looked where he was pointing, and it was only then that they noticed all the tires bobbing around in the water. Not that the tires weren't serving a useful purpose. There were lots of canoes and windsurfing boards stuck into them at odd angles and a fair number had people sprawled over them, shouting things. They caught sight of Tub drifting past with his eyes shut. He seemed to be pretty firmly wedged into his tire.

"Is he unconscious?" said Sharon.

"Only if you can be unconscious and chew at the same time," said George. "What do you think he's eating?"

"Fish?" said Stick.

"I don't think that French guy is shouting for help," said Julia.

They all looked. As they watched, the instructor yanked a windsurfing board out of a nearby tire and climbed aboard. It was really impressive the way he got going so quickly. Mostly people fall over first. He was getting up a lot of speed and he seemed to be coming straight at them. It was fairly safe to say it wasn't *help* he was shouting.

"Why is he mad at us?" said Stick.

There was a moment's pause, then they all looked at Kev, visible for miles in Day-Glo Bermudas and T-shirt, hanging one-handed over the side of the boat.

"What did you do?" said George.

"It started when he asked me to pull up that thing," said Kev.

"What thing?" said George, trying to keep an eye on the ever-nearer figure of the instructor. He looked like something bent on vengeance.

"This thing," said Kev, and brought his other hand out of the water. He was holding a dinghy's sailboard complete with rubber seal.

"Oh, that thing," said Stick. "I didn't know it came out."

"It doesn't," said Sharon, "at least the rubber seal doesn't."

The windsurfing board was getting nearer. If you could understand French, you'd have been able to make out what he was saying now. George was never more glad that he was rotten at French.

"Sharon," he said.

Sharon dragged her lasers away from Kev.

"What?"

"Can you drive this thing and park it somewhere quiet?"

"We didn't do anything," said Sharon.

"No, but we're going to," said George. "Get in, Kev."

"There isn't enough room," said Sharon.

"You can't leave him to be run over by a mad

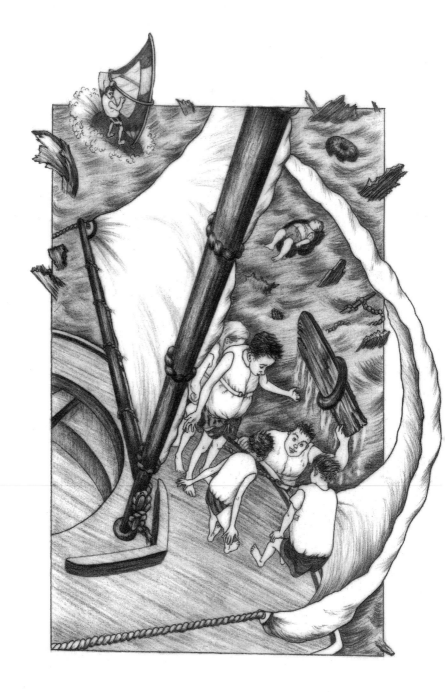

French windsurfer," said George. "Get in, Kev," he said again, but he was looking at Sharon.

For a moment the lasers flickered, then she said, "Aye, aye, sir."

He felt really good—sort of masterful—till she said, "And you don't drive it and park it, you sail it and berth it."

"I don't care if we have to paddle it with the 'noors,'" said George, "so long as it shifts fast enough."

They all leaned over the side of the boat to balance Kev getting in, then Sharon started shouting things at them. As far as George could see, sailing seemed to consist mainly of shouting. Sharon was good though. You had to hand it to her. She made Kev lie down in the middle of the boat and told him not to touch anything. The boat was a bit low in the water and definitely soggy in the bottom, but Kev was wet anyway. He didn't even seem to mind that they had to tramp all over him every time Sharon gave them an order. She gave them a lot of orders.

They beat the instructor to shore by a nose and were running as soon as their feet hit land.

"Where to?" said Stick.

"The village," George said. "We can't go back till the fuss dies down."

"We're here for four more days," said Julia. "How long will the fuss take to die down?"

You could always rely on Julia.

Aitken, George
Papillon sur Mer

12

George bought five Oranginas in the café they'd been to before in the village and plonked them down on a table—inside. Inside was safer. There was a television on in a corner, but nobody took any notice. It was in French. Even the pictures looked French. The screen was full of people on bicycles.

"What happened?" he said.

It was a long business. Getting information out of Kev was a matter of finding the right questions, and most of the things you had to ask weren't things you would have thought of asking in the first place.

"You mean before or after the boat crashed into the tires?" said Kev.

"Let's start with before," said George.

"Well, he was doing a lot of shouting," said Kev, "that instructor guy."

"That's what sailing's about," said George. "I bet they even get a certificate in shouting."

"In French," said Kev.

"And you couldn't understand it," said George.

Kev's eyebrows drew together, which was how you could tell he was thinking. "That's the funny thing," he said. "I could—some of it."

George was tempted to follow that up, but he resisted. First things first. They would get to Kev and the French language later.

"He was shouting," George prompted.

They had covered the capsize drill which, oddly enough, had gone like a dream, and got on to the part where the instructor was starting on basic sailing technique, when Tub walked in. "Thought I'd find you here," he said.

". . . So then he told us to pull that thing up," Kev was saying.

"He didn't mean you to pull it right out," said Tub. "I mean, once the rubber seal was off, the boat wasn't waterproof anymore, was it?"

"Tight," said Sharon.

Tub pulled at his T-shirt. "The label says it's my size," he said.

"No, I mean watertight," said Sharon, but Tub had gone to get some Orangina.

"Then what?" said George.

"He started yelling again," said Kev, "what do you think? So I tried to put it back, but it wouldn't fit so . . ."

George knew what was coming, "So you hammered it down."

It was a technique Kev was fond of.

"Yeah," said Kev, "with this thing off the back of the boat."

"The rudder," said Tub, coming back with his drink and a huge pancake, "the *raw dare*."

"You know," said Kev, "I don't think these boats are too safe. They're really flimsy."

"It was when he threw the rudder away and started stamping on the sailboard that the floor of the boat started to give way," said Tub.

"Why didn't you stop him?" said George.

"I was half over the side trying to get the rudder back," said Tub, "but it sank."

"Where was the instructor?" said Stick.

"Trying to get back into the boat," said Tub.

Julia was absentmindedly eating half his pancake.

"What was he doing in the water?" she said.

"Hanging on to this rope," said Tub.

"Sheet," said Sharon.

"That's what he was yelling," said Kev.

"How did he get into the water?" George said. Somebody had to get the facts.

"It was that pole thing. It kept swinging around," said Tub.

"Boom," said Sharon.

"Too right," said Tub. "What a bang it gave him. Still, it was okay once Kev tied it up."

"What did you tie it to?" said Sharon.

"There was another piece of rope where the rudder came off," said Kev. "You know, sailing's really dangerous."

"So what happened then?" said George.

Tub and Kev looked at each other and shrugged.

"That's when we started to go really fast," said Tub.

"The instructor slowed us down a bit," said Kev. "Without the drag of his weight, we'd definitely have gone faster."

"What? You mean he was still hanging on to the rope?" said Julia.

Tub chewed thoughtfully. "Not exactly," he said. "You see, he'd been showing us this harness thing you clip on to the side of the boat in bad weather in case you fall out."

"Overboard," said Sharon.

"He did go a bit over the edge," agreed Tub. "I mean, you could tell he was swearing even if it was in French."

"So why didn't you unclip him?" said Stick.

Tub looked offended. "Would I do a thing like

that?" he said. "He might have been drowned. We were pretty far out by that time."

"So what happened then?" said George. He felt like a broken record.

"The wind seemed to catch us a bit," said Tub. "It's breezy when you get right out there, isn't it, Kev? Kev?"

Kev was watching the TV. The cyclists had gone and a man was talking into the camera.

"Eh?" said Kev. "Somebody's kidnapped a tree."

There was a short silence. Kev was fond of trees.

"Probably a concussion," Julia said. "Ignore him."

"Okay," said Tub. "Anyway, the wind seemed to get right under us, and I'm nearly sure we weren't even touching the water. It was just a pity about those tires."

"You hit them?" said Stick.

"More sort of bounced off them," said Tub, "but with the floor of the boat being a bit mangled by then, the whole thing sort of went to pieces. It was the instructor who actually hit the tires. He was more in the water than we were."

George was puzzled. "I don't see how that can happen," he said, "even to you."

"I do," Sharon interrupted. "With the boom tied to the helm and no sailboard, if the wind caught you, you'd just aquaplane before it. No control. No control at all."

"That instructor didn't have any control," said Tub. Then, as if he'd been reminded of something, "Mr. Martin sent me to find you."

"It was nothing to do with us," said Sharon.

"He said you aided and abetted Kev's escape," said Tub. "He also said he made a deal with George."

"Why me?" said George. "Why does it always have to be my fault? Even when I'm not there."

"You could have left Kev," said Julia.

George looked at Kev, immersed in French television.

"No, I couldn't," he said. "Come on, Kev."

"What was this deal Mr. Martin made with you, George?" said Sharon as they trudged back along the road toward camp.

"Oh, just that I'm responsible for these guys," said George. "They get into trouble, it's my fault."

"That doesn't sound very fair," said Sharon.

George didn't say anything. After all, it was why he decided in the first place that he just had to come on this trip, wasn't it? It was why he'd fixed it— wasn't it?

"Well, I'm certainly not responsible for them," Sharon was saying.

George looked at her. They had all been soaked to the skin but, whereas the rest of them looked as if they'd been hung out on a line to dry, Sharon gave the impression she'd been sent to the dry cleaners.

113

Perfection—and she hated getting into trouble.

"No, you aren't," said George, "and I'll tell Mr. Martin that."

Sharon smiled at him and he stopped trudging.

Protective, that's how he felt, and it wasn't very often Sharon Taylor gave anybody the chance to feel like that.

Even when Kev said "How can you kidnap a tree?" all George said was "Give it a rest, Kev."

Kindly, that's how he was feeling. He even managed to ignore Julia's muttering about saps and traitors.

"You can almost see his shining armor," Stick said, looking at George disgustedly. "Met any good dragons lately, George?"

"If he hasn't, he's going to," said Tub. "Mr. Bell saw the whole thing."

George started trudging again. He was still trudging as they crossed the compound. It was getting more and more like that film Tub's mom watched every Christmas. Nobody whistled this time.

They were lucky, at least, luckier than they might have been. It was Mr. Martin and Jenny who were waiting for them in the camp director's office, and every time Mr. Martin started shouting, Jenny said, "Oh, Giles," and he stopped.

Julia loved it. Mr. Martin ended up having to conduct the entire conversation in a kind of hoarse roar.

"They've had to mount a rescue operation," he said. "They've got a helicopter out there."

"I've always wanted to ride in a helicopter," said Tub.

"How did you get back to shore anyway?" said George.

"The camp director sent someone out to tow him in," said Mr. Martin.

"They wouldn't let me in the boat," said Tub.

"Are you surprised?" Mr. Martin was roaring again.

"Oh, Giles," said Jenny, and gave Tub a fruit drop. They all clustered around Jenny. It seemed the safest place to be.

"Do you realize the chaos you caused?" said Mr. Martin in a strangulated voice.

"We got a fair idea," said Tub, and crunched his fruit drop.

"Tell you what," said Kev, "nobody's getting me in a boat again. Boats are dangerous."

It was a moment before Mr. Martin could speak at all.

"You won't be allowed in a boat again," he said. "You won't get near a boat. You'll be lucky if you're allowed to have a shower, you'll be so far from water. Water is out of bounds."

"Suits me," said Tub before Jenny shoveled a few more fruit drops into him to shut him up.

"It wasn't all bad," said Stick. "My T-shirt is really clean now."

"Mom will be pleased about that when she hears," said Julia sarcastically.

It was pretty hot in the camp director's office, but Sharon's voice brought the temperature down quite a bit.

"George," she said.

George snapped to attention. "It has nothing to do with Sharon," he said. "I told her to let Kev into the boat."

Mr. Martin was trying to get past Jenny to reach Tub, but he stopped at that.

"Told her?" he said.

"Told her," said George proudly.

"Now, Giles," Jenny said.

Mr. Martin gave George a considering look.

"Remind me to have a talk with you," he said.

"Mr. Martin . . ." said Sharon.

"I don't blame you, Sharon," Mr. Martin said. "I didn't for a moment blame you, and now I see you were forced into doing what you did." He didn't sound as if he believed what he was saying.

George thought it was time to change the subject. "Where's Mr. Bell?" he said.

"Gone to help direct the rescue operation," said Mr. Martin. "Somebody gave him a whistle."

"I think you should stay out of Mr. Bell's way for a while, Kev," said Jenny. "He isn't too pleased."

Mr. Martin ran a hand through his hair. "Not too pleased? He's foaming at the mouth."

George nearly said, "Now, Giles," but Jenny got there before him.

"Bikes," said Mr. Martin.

"We never touched them," said Julia.

"Bikes," Mr. Martin repeated. "That's your special interest. All except Sharon. You're all on bikes from now on. You like bikes. You love bikes. Bikes are your all-consuming passion."

"Why bikes?" said Julia.

"Because bikes don't go in the water," Mr. Martin said. "Bikes are definitely dry land only and bikes will get you out of camp and out of Mr. Bell's way."

"I like bikes," said Stick. "I even brought my cycling helmet."

"It's supposed to be a punishment," said Mr. Martin, and Jenny started saying how nice it was to see them making the best of things. Mr. Martin was clearly reconsidering bikes and trying to think of something they would hate, when a freshman stuck her head around the door.

"Sir, Mr. Bell says can you come and help. They've had to call the helicopter off and there are still some people who need rescuing."

"Why have they called the helicopter off?" said Mr. Martin. The freshman shrugged. "Mr. Bell said it had to go to a kidnapping."

She made it sound like a party the way she said it.

Mr. Martin looked at them, and they all took one step backward. Jenny got another "Now, Giles" in before dragging him away.

"They aren't responsible for everything that happens," they heard her say as she led him out the door.

"George," said Sharon, "I appreciate your speaking up for me, but if you get into any more trouble, I shall have to ask for the return of the Andalusian hunchback. I cannot allow the society to associate itself with rowdy elements," she finished as she walked out.

George stood staring after her. What a disgrace, he thought. Stripped of his pig badge. No longer fit for the Friends of the Animals society. If he didn't watch out, he'd be back to being an amoeba.

"Where did she learn to talk like that?" said Stick.

Julia was capering around. *"The Return of the Andalusian Hunchback,"* she squawked. "Is it on video yet?"

"What's an Andalusian hunchback?" said Tub.

"Must be the tree," said Kev.

"No, it isn't. It's a pig," said Stick.

George left them and walked out the door, miserable. He looked down on the bay. A few tires were still floating around, and he could see some kids being hauled into a boat. Somebody somewhere was blowing a whistle.

Aitken, George
Papillon sur Mer

13

Stick was the only one who was pleased about the bikes. He loved bikes. He was always fiddling around with his racer at home. He'd even brought his cycling shorts and his helmet with him. Seeing Stick at full pelt on his racing bike was something else. He looked like a motorized spider. He turned up the next morning looking like nothing on earth. He was wearing his bright yellow T-shirt with his cycling shorts. Yellow definitely did not suit Stick. Kev was wearing an even brighter pair of Bermudas and he looked better than Stick. George shaded his eyes. So long as he didn't ride behind them, the dazzle effect wouldn't be too bad.

"Jenny's coming with us," said Julia.

"I thought Mr. Martin said we could go off on our own," said Tub.

"The camp director wouldn't allow it," said Julia. "Too risky."

Mr. Martin appeared around the corner. "Jenny's going with you," he said.

George nodded. "Julia's just told us." He carefully didn't ask the question. Mr. Martin answered it anyway.

"She volunteered," he said. "I've got to supervise canoeing today, so look, you guys . . ." That was as far as he got. Jenny appeared, said, "Oh, Giles," and shepherded them off to the bike huts.

"Funny-looking bikes," said Tub when he saw them.

Stick was in among them. "Mountain bikes," he said. "Terrific. I've been wanting to try one of these. They've got about twenty gears and the frame is made of aluminum. They're so light you can carry them, no bother."

"What's the point in carrying a bike?" said Julia. "I thought the idea of a bike was that it carried you."

"With these," said Stick, patting one of them lovingly, "you can climb mountains. Into an incredibly low gear and it'll take anything."

"Nobody said anything about mountains," said Tub.

Jenny smiled. "Don't worry, Tub. We'll be sticking to the roads—for today, at any rate," she added, seeing the disappointment on Stick's face.

"Right," said Mr. Martin. "Who's got a knapsack?" Nobody owned up.

"Come on," said Mr. Martin. "One of you must have a knapsack."

"What do we need a knapsack for?" said George.

"To carry the packed lunches and the first aid kit," said Mr. Martin.

"We haven't got a first aid kit," said George.

"You will have," said Mr. Martin grimly. "If you think I'm letting you out of this camp without a first aid kit . . ."

"Julia's got one," said Stick, "a knapsack, not a first aid kit."

Julia rounded on him furiously. "Shut up, Stick."

"Gran gave it to her to bring on vacation," said Stick, and followed it up with a few ouches as Julia connected with him.

The rest of them stood around expectantly.

"Get the knapsack, Julia," said Mr. Martin.

Julia gave Stick a look that should have felled him on the spot and slouched off around the side of the hut.

By the time she came back, they had the bikes assigned.

"I'll report you to Sharon's Friends of the Animals," said George as Julia handed the knapsack over to Mr. Martin.

"I think it's sweet," said Jenny, "but isn't it a bit big, Julia?"

Julia was looking daggers at Stick.

"She made it," said Stick. "Our gran. At her handicrafts class."

"Ah," said Jenny, and looked understandingly at Julia. "It's very well made. Strong," she said. "I wonder if my aunt would be interested in handicrafts classes. What do you think, Giles?"

Mr. Martin went pale. "It would make a change from free-fall parachuting," he said.

They had all met Jenny's aunt.

"I thought it was karate," said George.

"Not exciting enough," said Mr. Martin.

Tub was looking at the knapsack. "What is it?" he said. "A gorilla?"

"It's supposed to be a panda," said Julia. "She drew the pattern herself."

"Pandas are black and white," said Tub. "That's brown and sort of moldy green."

"They didn't have any black-and-white fur coats at the senior citizens rummage sale," said Stick.

"Looks more like a gorilla to me," said Tub. "It's big enough."

Mr. Martin unzipped the knapsack and the head

fell back and leered at them. Whatever it was, it was extremely furry, the bits that weren't molting. Mr. Martin dropped the first aid kit in and it fell with a thud to the bottom of the knapsack.

"Teeth?" he said. "Do pandas have teeth? I suppose they do."

"Gran's old ones," said Stick. "She hates waste. She said she kept seeing a lot of girls with animal knapsacks and she thought Julia would like one."

"Mom made me bring it," said Julia.

Mr. Martin zipped it up again, and the head snapped back. The teeth clashed.

"Quite right," said Mr. Martin. "After all, she made it for you." He took another look at it. "I think Tub's right. Definitely a gorilla. You carry it, Kev."

If George hadn't made up his mind before, he definitely had now. There was no way he was riding behind Kev with a gorilla on his back.

As they were getting ready to leave, Sharon passed by.

"Don't suppose you relish a day out on mountain bikes?" said George.

Her eyes rested on the knapsack, and the lasers flashed. She passed by without a word. George sighed. "Where are we going, then?"

"I thought Auray," said Jenny. "The Tour de France finishes one of its stages there today. It should be interesting."

"What's the Tour de France?" said Kev. His accent was surprisingly good. The gorilla nodded over his shoulder.

"Only the most famous cycling race in the world," said Stick. "It lasts for weeks. It goes all over France." He tightened up his helmet. "Suits me."

The bikes were quite different from any they had ridden before and, once you got used to all the gears, pretty terrific. They were made so that you had to sit forward more than usual and the brakes were really sharp, but they were great for going uphill. Stick was right. In a low gear you could climb anything.

It was quite a long way to Auray, and George began to suspect Jenny of deliberately choosing somewhere that would keep them out of camp all day and tire them out. They ate their packed lunches early in the day, mainly because of Tub. As he said, it was less to carry—as if he were carrying anything in the first place. As they got nearer to Auray, they noticed a lot of policemen and motorbikes and what looked like film crews lining the road. Some men in Day-Glo armbands were setting up barriers across the side roads. They stopped at the top of the hill leading down to the river that ran through the town.

"What was all that about?" said Tub.

"The race," Jenny said. "They've got to get the

road cleared well before the cyclists come through. Auray is the end of a stage, so it's pretty important. They won't be here for quite a while yet, but I thought we could explore the town and be here on the spot for the leader's arrival."

"See who gets the yellow jersey," said Stick.

"The what?" said Julia.

"The leader at each stage gets a yellow shirt to wear," said Stick, "and he wears it for the next stage."

"Why?" said Julia.

"I don't know, do I?" said Stick. "Tradition, I imagine, or so the people watching can tell who's in the lead."

Jenny was looking down toward the town. "Isn't it picturesque?" she said.

It was. The hill leading down into the town was pretty steep, in fact extremely steep. It curved around, crossing an old stone bridge over a river. There were people perched on the bridge fishing, and beyond the bridge the road opened out into a kind of square with cafés and shops on two sides. The other side was river. It came up almost to the road.

"It's a tidal river," said Jenny. "When the tide is in, the water can come right on to the road. That's the Saint Gustan quarter. There are lots of lovely fifteenth-century houses there."

The buildings rose steeply behind the square, a

mass of houses with shutters closed against the sun. Church towers stuck up higgledy-piggledy all over the place.

"Awful lot of churches," said George.

Jenny smiled. "Yes, aren't there? I thought we might look at a few of them. The early Romanesque architecture is particularly interesting. You'll enjoy it. It's educational."

George looked at Tub. "Your dad would be pleased," he said as Jenny set off down the hill.

"Churches," said Tub. "You've got to do something, George."

George was still shouting things like "why me?" at him as they free-wheeled into the café opposite the river.

"Some hill that was," said Stick, unclamping his helmet.

Kev's gorilla was looking a bit windblown. Its head rested on his shoulder. Julia's gran's teeth grinned.

George sat down beside Jenny at a table on the sidewalk.

"About these churches," he began, but Jenny was busy giving orders for drinks.

Kev and the gorilla followed the waiter into the café. The rest of them gathered around and sat down at the table. Tub amused himself twirling the umbrella around and around.

"About these churches . . ." George tried again, but all that produced was a ten-minute talk on Franco-Roman architecture from Jenny. Once she got going she really could talk. George began to see how it worked with Kev's dad. She came to a stop when their drinks came.

"What on earth has happened to Kev?" she said.

"He went into the café," said Tub.

Stick grinned. "Maybe they don't serve gorillas."

"I'll go and see," said George.

It was cool and dark in the café and the TV was on. Kev and the gorilla were watching it with exactly the same expression on their faces. George glanced at the screen before starting to shout at Kev, and then suddenly shouting at Kev was the last thing on his mind.

"It's that kid," he said, "the one on the ferry."

"Tamarind," said Kev. "It's a tree."

"So you said," said George.

The picture changed as he watched, and another photograph flashed up. It was the man in the leather jacket. Somebody was babbling French in the background.

"He was with her," said George.

"It's that kidnapping thing I was telling you about," said Kev.

George was puzzled. He couldn't make out a word. He looked from Kev to the gorilla and decided it was marginally more useful talking to Kev.

"Can you understand what they're saying?" he said.

"Bits," said Kev.

"So who's the guy?"

"I don't know," said Kev. "I didn't get that. You know, George, I don't think it's a tree that's been kidnapped after all."

Things were beginning to make sense to George. The kid had said she was being kidnapped, but who would believe that? She didn't look as if anybody was kidnapping her. She wasn't tied up or gagged or anything. She was just a kid with a good imagination—or so he had thought. He'd thought of that kid since then. When? On the traffic circle with the Rosalie when that black car had nearly demolished them. Why should that make him think of the kid? Then he remembered waking up on that bus trip to the camp and seeing that guy take her out of one car and put her in another one—a big black one with smoked glass windows. Maybe that was when she was kidnapped. But how come she knew on the ferry? It didn't make sense. Or maybe he'd been dreaming that bit about the car. He couldn't even be sure he'd been awake. And Kev talking about somebody kidnapping a tree. He'd ignored that. That was normal enough. You couldn't afford to listen to everything Kev said and hold on to your sanity at the same time. The TV screen changed and was filled with men in cycling shorts and helmets and T-shirts zipping along on bikes. The Tour de France.

"Jenny's wondering where you've gone to," he said to Kev. "Come on."

"It wasn't a tree, it was a kid," Kev said when they sat down at the table.

"Anything you say, Kev," said Tub.

Jenny looked as if she was going to try to find out what Kev was talking about, so George started asking her about churches. He had to think about this. He supposed he should go to the police and tell them what he saw—thought he saw—but it would sound bad enough in English, and his French didn't get past "pardon"—pronounced either way. Maybe Kev could help. He seemed to be able to understand bits of French. It was weird. He'd have to get to the bottom of that. Jenny then. He rehearsed the story in his mind while she went on and on about plinths and arches. It couldn't help, he thought. They obviously knew the kid was in France and they had a photo of the guy. How could he help? He'd probably get a flea in his ear for wasting police time while they were all busy with this bike race. It was the helicopter that clinched it. That freshman telling Mr. Martin the helicopter had to go to a kidnapping. What good would his story do if they had helicopters on the job? They'd probably caught the guy by now.

He was so immersed in finding excuses not to get involved that they were in their first church before he realized it. They had left the bikes at the café. Tub was in a bad mood. Tub didn't often lose his temper, so it was bad when he did. George could see him getting worse with each church.

"I thought you were going to do something," he hissed at George as they crammed into the third one.

"Why can't you do something?" said George. "Use your initiative. I've got other things on my mind." He looked around. "Anyway, this one isn't so bad. It's easily the best yet. It's got tinsel and flashing lights. More like a disco than a church really. It's a lot brighter than those other two."

It was true. The other two had been what you'd expect from an old church. Boring. This one was different. It looked as if somebody had had a party in it. There was hardly an inch of it that wasn't garishly painted and illuminated with hundreds of tiny little electric bulbs. There was even a touch of neon here and there. Jenny was having difficulty with this one. You could tell from the way she was hanging over the font, blinking at the lights. Piped music suddenly switched itself on and she gave up.

"You continue to look around," she said. "I'll just

go outside for a moment. If we should get separated, we'll meet back at the café for the Tour de France coming through."

"Music even," said George to Tub. "What more do you want?"

"What other things?" said Tub.

"What?" said George.

"On what you call your mind?" said Tub.

Julia, Stick, and Kev had gathered around.

"Is there a back door out of here?" said Julia. "I'm all for getting separated."

"What other things?" said Tub.

When Tub got into a bad mood, you wished he would do it more often and then it wouldn't seem so bad when it did happen.

"It sounds ridiculous," said George. "I can't even be sure if some of it happened."

"I feel like that sometimes," said Stick. "Usually after Mom's been giving me a hard time."

George plunged into the story with a bit of help from Kev.

"You're right," said Tub when he'd finished. "It does sound ridiculous."

"George," said Julia. "George."

But George was staring past her. They all turned and looked. A very small person was standing on a plinth at the far end of the church. George knew it was a plinth. Jenny had told him in detail about

great plinths she had known and loved. You saw
visions in churches, didn't you? It, the person not
the plinth, wasn't wearing a micro biker's jacket and
tour T-shirt and jeans. It was wearing a frilly blue
dress and was staring at Kev in a fixed manner.
Around it lights flashed and winked. It was the kid,
Tamarind.

"You've got two heads," she said to Kev.

"That's her," said George and, to the kid, "You're
supposed to be kidnapped."

The kid flounced out her frills. "This is my kidnap
dress," she said.

George's head swam. Maybe that freshman had been right. Maybe a kidnapping was a new kind of party after all. Maybe this was where the party was. A deep voice sounded from behind a pillar.

"Tamarind, put these things on. We've got to go now. Somebody might come in," and the guy in the leather jacket appeared around the pillar.

For a moment everybody stood perfectly still. They looked at the guy. The guy looked at them. Tamarind and the gorilla looked at each other. Then the guy moved like lightning. He crammed a wide floppy hat over the kid's hair, threw a jacket around her, and picked her up, making for the door.

"Head him off," yelled George before he knew what he was saying, and they were after him.

Twice around the church, in and out of the pillars they raced. It was unfortunate that they all approached him from different directions. Good tactics but too much speed. They met with a combined crunch. Kev nearly got him but, as he reached out to grab the guy, he was suddenly yanked backward. The gorilla had caught on the handle of a small cupboard. He hauled it off, and the handle came with it, and he staggered back with the sudden release. The cupboard was full of little boxes with buttons on them, set into the wall. Kev hit every one of the buttons squarely. Immediately, lights began flashing even more dementedly, the neon sprang into new and glowing life, and the piped music swelled to meet the pain barrier. Every statue, cross, and picture in the place pulsed with color, and the tinsel started to vibrate. Tamarind squealed with delight just before the guy in the leather jacket, his face reflecting the glow of a thousand tiny lights, gave a low moan and fled out of the door.

They were on their feet, disentangled in record time, but getting stuck in the door as they all tried to get through at once didn't help. George caught sight of Jenny's face as they raced past with him, yelling at them to keep the guy in sight.

"Can't stop," he shouted to Jenny. "Meet you in the café later."

He hurtled after the others down the steep, twisty, narrow, cobbled lane. Just their luck. Any one of those wouldn't have been so bad, but steep, twisty, narrow, *and* cobbled was a bit much.

They were just emerging from the lane onto the square when George saw the big black car with the smoked glass windows driving away. He absolutely hadn't been dreaming that night on the bus.

"Get the bikes," he shouted.

"Then what?" said Julia, pounding along breathlessly beside him.

"What do you think?" said George. "Follow that car."

He'd always wanted to say that.

Aitken, George
Papillon sur Mer

14

Following the car was easier said than done. It shot up the hill as if it had never heard of gravity. By the time they got to the top, they were exhausted. The bikes might be built for mountains, but they still depended on pedal power. George slumped over the handlebars, gasping. Kev wasn't even out of breath. Kev was amazingly fit. Stick and Julia weren't looking too fit, but Tub had the situation well in hand. He arrived at the top last of all and simply fell off his bike. He lay there at the side of the road with his mouth open, staring glassily at the sky.

"Where's he gone, then?" said Kev.

George looked around. There was a knot of people about fifty yards away, where a side road joined the main road. They seemed to be replacing barriers.

"There's a policeman over there," said Julia.

"A French policeman," said George. "How's your French?"

"I can ask for a ticket to the movies," said Julia.

"Oh, big deal," said George. "That's going to help a lot."

There was nothing else to do. He knew that.

"We'll have to try to tell that policeman," he said. "What's French for 'kidnap'?"

The other three looked at him blankly. Tub was still looking at the sky—blankly.

"Come on, Kev," said George.

"I can't speak French," said Kev.

George looked at him, puzzled. "No, but you seem to be able to understand it."

Kev put up a hand to scratch his head and scratched the gorilla's by mistake. It didn't seem to mind.

"Bits," he said.

"Bits is better than nothing," said George. "Come on."

Maybe it was his accent. He got a couple of words right—like *fille* and *homme* and even *automobile*, but the policeman kept having to drag his eyes away

136

from Kev's gorilla. George got the feeling he wasn't paying attention. When he did speak, he did a lot of arm waving and the words came out with the speed of machine-gun bullets. George began to feel they couldn't have been worse off with Julia and her movie tickets. Then he got an idea. If they couldn't tell him, they could demonstrate.

"Julia."

"What?"

"Come here and be kidnapped."

George thought the pantomime was quite good. They had done role play in drama at school. They all thought it was good—all except Tub. He was still concentrating on minor things like breathing. And Julia, who was being kidnapped. She didn't seem to think it was very good. In his enthusiasm, George wasn't being too gentle about it. Miss Cox, the drama teacher, always said you had to throw yourself heart and soul into the part.

"Let me go," Julia was yelling.

"That's it," said George. "Now struggle a bit. Really get the feel of the part."

She kicked him on the shin.

"Ow," said George. "No need to overdo it."

Julia might be small, but she was a fair enough fighter. George slung her over his shoulder, ran around a bit, then turned around and put her down.

"See?" he yelled to the policeman. "Like that."

The policeman started to yell back.

"What's he saying, Kev?" said George.

Kev was concentrating hard. His eyes were nearly invisible under his eyebrows. "I think he's going to arrest us, George."

"Terrific," said George. "Try to help the police, and you get arrested."

"Wait a minute," said Kev.

"What?" said George.

"He's talking about some car and the bike race and the barriers. I think he's pretty fed up."

Tub arrived beside George.

"Had a nice rest?" said George.

"Did you do that?" said Tub.

George looked where Tub was looking. Three men in Day-Glo armbands were trying to piece a broken barrier together. The policeman marched up to them and started to wave his arms around. He was talking again. The men waved back.

"No," said George, "but it doesn't take much imagination to guess who did. Let's go."

"What about the policeman?" said Kev.

"He doesn't want to know, does he?" said George. "It's up to us."

"Be fair, George," said Kev. "He's having a hard day and his back's acting up again."

George shook his head in wonder. "How is it you can understand it but not speak it? How is it you can understand it at all?"

"I don't know," said Kev. "Funny, isn't it?"

"They aren't going to be too happy if we crash through their barrier," said Stick.

"It's broken already, isn't it?" said George. "Anyway, we don't have to. We'll go around it. Mountain bikes, remember?"

They cut across the corner of the field beside the road.

"Are you sure he went this way?" said Julia.

"That broken barrier is the only lead we've got," said George.

"How do you think we're going to find him?" said Tub. "He'll be miles away by now."

"Maybe," said George, "but we've got to try. Wave to the policeman."

They all waved to the policeman as they thumped back onto the road. He was jumping up and down and flailing his arms at them.

"What's he saying, Kev?"

Kev looked puzzled. "I can make out some of the words, but I don't see how you can do that to a person."

"Forget it," said George. "I don't think I want to know."

Half an hour later they were still pedaling. The road had led them steadily away from the town and into the countryside. Julia was riding beside George.

"We'll never find him," she said, "and even if we do, what are we going to do about it?"

"Look," said George, "it's not as if anybody else knows where she is. I mean, it looks like it's up to us, doesn't it? There haven't been any other roads off this one. If he came this way, we're on his trail."

"If," said Tub from behind him.

George braked, and the rest drew up beside him.

"Say we do find him," said Stick, "what are we going to do then? Arrest him? Excuse me, you're caught. Would you mind giving yourself up?"

George looked at Kev. "What do you say, Kev?"

Kev put his head on one side and the gorilla nuzzled his left ear. "She's just a little kid," he said.

George looked around at the rest of the faces. Kev had said it all.

"Who said anything about giving up?" said Tub.

"Even if we don't arrest him, we can at least try to find out where he's taking her," said Stick.

"You never know your luck," said Julia.

"Luck?" said George. "You make your own."

He looked around.

"Kev," he said, "what are you doing up there?"

Kev and the gorilla were straddling the roof of one of those little shrines that stand at the side of the road all over Brittany. The statue of the saint underneath it didn't look too happy. Maybe it was a martyr.

"Lookout post," said Kev. "It's pretty flat around here. I can see for miles."

"See what?" said Stick.

"Fields," said Kev, "and trees . . . and wait a minute."

He lurched to his feet, balancing on the pointed roof of the shrine. It was like a miniature house, a bit like a fancy bird-table. The saint wobbled.

"And?" said Tub.

Kev swayed. The gorilla bobbed about on his shoulder, getting quite excited.

"And a big . . ." said Kev before he fell off and crashed into the hedge at the side of the road. There was a split second before the statue fell on top of him. It was a bit bad-tempered–looking, which seemed odd for a saint. Kev and the gorilla lay there with the saint between them.

"And a big black car with smoked glass windows," said Kev.

"Where?" They were on him, dragging him to his feet.

Kev brushed bits of hedge off himself, the gorilla, and the saint. "I wonder who it's supposed to be," he said, looking at it.

"Never mind that," said George. "Where's the car?"

Kev put the saint back in its little house and added a few leaves for decoration. "About three fields away," he said. "There's a building. You can hardly see it for trees, but the car is there."

"Just out in the open?" said Stick.

"Sort of half sticking out of a barn," said Kev.

"Why leave it where it can be seen?" said Tub.

"Probably couldn't get it all in," Stick said. "Serves him right for having such a big, flashy car."

"Okay," said George, "so how do we get there?"

"We've got to follow the road anyway," said Julia. "It's the only one. If there's a turn, we're bound to see it."

But they didn't. Not the first time. They had to double back and, when they did find it, they realized why they had missed it before. It wasn't really a road, just a dirt track, and so overgrown you could hardly believe a car could get down it. On their bikes it was no problem, but bumpy.

"How on earth did he manage to get that car down here?" said Stick.

"That's probably the point," said Tub. "Nobody would think of coming down this path to look for a car."

The trees and bushes began to thin out, and they got off the bikes, shoved them into a hedge out of sight, and crept forward. Quite suddenly they came up on an open space with a house in the middle. It was an old farmhouse built of gray stone. All the shutters were closed.

"It looks deserted," said Tub.

"There's the car," said Julia, "sticking out of that barn. They must be here."

"So what do we do?" said Stick. "George?"

George had a faraway look on his face.

"Shut up," said Julia. "He's thinking."

George spoke, "If we were commandos, we'd just crash in and grab the kid."

"But we're not commandos," said Stick. "Is that the best you can do?"

"You've got to look at this problem logically," said George. "First things first. We've got to immobilize the car. Even if we can't rescue the kid, we can make sure that guy has to stay put. Who knows anything about cars?"

Nobody did.

"They never teach you anything useful at school," George grumbled.

"In any case, we'd need tools if we were going to do anything to the car," said Stick. "All we've got is a lousy first aid kit."

George's eyes lit up.

"There might be something in it we can use." He unzipped the knapsack on Kev's back and the gorilla's head lolled back. "Why did she put the zipper in the neck?" he asked as he hauled the first aid kit out.

"Who knows with our gran?" said Stick. "What's in it?"

They searched through the box. Adhesive tape, antiseptic, bandages, scissors, tweezers, bite cream, sting cream, insect repellent, and a bottle of aspirin. They looked at the pile in dismay.

"We could always cut the tires to ribbons with the scissors," said Tub.

"They're only about three inches long," said Stick. "You'd be lucky if you could cut the bandages with them."

"Don't they usually have tubes in first aid kits?" said Julia.

"There are tubes," said George. "Sting cream and stuff."

"No, I mean just plastic tubes."

"Why tubes?" said Tub.

"Tubes are sort of medical, aren't they?" said Julia. "You see them all over people on TV programs about hospitals. This is a rotten first aid kit."

"What do you want a tube for?" said George.

"If we had a tube, we could siphon off the gasoline," said Julia.

"She's right," said Kev.

"She might be," said George, "but we don't have a tube. Good idea though, Julia," he added, and his voice trailed off.

"He's thinking again," said Stick.

"Didn't do much good last time," said Tub. "Anybody want some lemon sherbet?" He held out a bag full of yellow powder.

"That's it!" said George.

"What?" said Stick.

"We put it in the gas tank."

"What?" said Stick again.

"Everything," said George. He grabbed Tub's paper bag. "Even this."

"What for?" said Julia.

"I was enjoying that," said Tub.

"Look," said George, "if we stuff all this in the gas tank, it's bound to do something to the car. I mean, you can't drive around with a first aid kit and lemon sherbet in your tank and expect it not to have an effect. Stands to reason."

"You're sure you need the sherbet?" said Tub.

George looked at him. "We need everything," he said.

Julia looked hopefully at the gorilla.

"Forget it," said George. "It wouldn't fit. All right, you guys, let's go—and quietly."

"We should go one at a time," said Stick.

"Why?" said Tub.

"So that we can keep each other covered," said Stick.

Julia gave him a look.

"What with?" she said. "The tweezers?"

They crept across the farmyard in single file and gathered around the car on the side farthest from the house.

"The gas-tank cap is on the other side," said Stick.

"It would be," said Tub. "Just our luck."

"We'll have to risk it," said George. "Come on."

They crept around the car once more and Tub got the cap off.

"Right," said George, and opened the bottle of antiseptic.

It glugged into the gas tank, making a terrible racket. They followed it up with the scissors, the bandages, the tape, the tweezers, and the aspirin.

They even squirted the sting cream, the bite cream, and the insect repellent in. George pried the lemon sherbet out of Tub's hands again. "It's for a good cause," he said as he poured it into the tank.

"What now?" said Stick.

"Now we find the kid," said George.

"What are you doing to the car?" said a voice behind him.

"Oh, for goodness' sake, I told you . . ." he said before he recognized the voice.

Tamarind was standing behind them, playing with the frills on her dress. For a moment none of them could speak, and George just managed to stop Stick from grabbing her.

"You'll frighten her," he said.

"I'm not frightened," said Tamarind. Her voice was one of those annoying kid's voices—really high and loud.

"Shhhh," said George.

"Why?" said Tamarind in a deafening whisper.

"Just because," said George.

"Just because why?" said Tamarind.

George wondered why on earth anybody would want to kidnap her.

"Because it's a secret," said George.

"I've got a secret," said Tamarind. "Do you want to know it?"

"Sure," said George.

"I can wear nice dresses because I'm kidnapped."

"She doesn't seem to mind being kidnapped," said Julia.

"Probably too young to understand," said Stick.

George had a brainstorm. "Would you like to be kidnapped again?" he said.

Tamarind thought about it. "No," she said. "I'm kidnapped already."

George thought maybe Stick had been right and they should just grab her, but if they did, she'd probably scream the place down. She put out a hand and stroked Kev's gorilla.

"I like him," she said.

"Do you like bikes?" said George.

"I like trains," she said.

George was losing patience. "Look," he said, "we haven't got a train. We've got bikes and we want you to come for a ride on our bikes with us."

She thought again. She seemed to be the kind of kid who did a lot of thinking.

"Okay," she said.

George nearly fell over with surprise.

"No wonder she got herself kidnapped," said Tub. "Didn't anybody ever tell her she shouldn't go with strangers?"

"People that age never have any sense," said Stick.

"Shut up and don't knock it," said George. "Come on, kid."

"I want to go with him," said Tamarind.

She was pointing to Kev, or maybe it was the gorilla. Who could tell? She reached up and her hand disappeared in Kev's massive one. Kev seemed quite pleased.

"You're a tree," he said.

"No, I'm not," she said. "I'm a chatterbox."

"Now, look," said George, "er . . . Tamarind. We've got to be very quiet."

"Why?" said Tamarind.

"It's a game," said George. "A very quiet game."

"Why?" said Tamarind.

"It just is," said George, "so no talking."

"Can I sing?" she said. "I like singing. My daddy sings."

George remembered her talking about her dad. He wore tiny T-shirts and used to be really big. Okay, so her dad was a singing dwarf. He could handle that. Everybody had to make a living somehow. It didn't mean her dad wouldn't be worried about her.

"No," he snapped. "You can't sing or talk or make any kind of noise till we get to the bikes."

"Why?" said Tamarind.

"If we hadn't put the sherbet in the tank, we could have bribed her with it," said Tub.

"If we hadn't put the adhesive tape in the tank, we could have sealed her mouth up," said George.

"Tamarind," said Julia, "if you're really quiet till we get to the bikes, you can sing all you like then. Okay?"

Tamarind thought. "Okay," she said.

She was a weird kid.

They scuttled across the farmyard into the bushes where they had left the bikes, and it was only then that the problem occurred to them.

"Where are we going to put her?" said Julia.

The bike crossbars were no go. You had to sit too

far forward to be able to carry anybody there, and there wasn't a rack on the back.

"The handlebars?" said Tub.

"She'd fall off," said Tub.

"Somebody could give her a piggyback," said Julia. "What's that noise?"

They looked around. Tamarind was singing. It was diabolical. Behind the horrendous noise they heard the sound of a door opening and a voice shouting.

"Tamarind!"

"It's him," said Julia.

George looked from the kid in the frilly dress— she was dancing as well as singing—to Stick, to Julia, to Tub, to Kev. Nobody looked helpful. He turned to the gorilla in despair. Its head lolled back from the gaping hole of its insides and grinned at him.

"In the gorilla," he said. "Put her in there."

"What?" said Julia, but George had already picked up Tamarind.

"Bend down, Kev."

He stuffed her feet into the knapsack and she sat there, her frilly blue dress fanned out around her, clutching the gorilla's head. She was still singing.

A figure appeared, racing across the farmyard, and stopped in disbelief at the sight of Tamarind singing to the gorilla. She waved at the man in the leather jacket as Kev staggered to his feet.

"On the bikes," yelled George.

They scrambled for the bikes and were already pedaling as the guy in the leather jacket pounded toward them, hesitated, changed his mind, and raced back toward the barn. The last thing they heard as they bucketed down the lane was the protesting cough of an engine trying to cope with a new experience, and the sound of Tamarind singing.

Aitken, George
Papillon sur Mer

15

They shot out of the lane and onto the road. Stick was in front, pedaling like mad, and it was a few moments before George realized they were heading in the wrong direction.

"Hey," he shouted. "That's the wrong way. We want to go back to Auray."

Stick had his head down. He didn't appear to hear. Kev turned briefly, trying to see between the heads of Tamarind and the gorilla, and nearly went into the ditch. Tub pedaled up beside George with Julia following.

"No good," he said. "Guess who's behind us?"

George looked back. The nose of the big black car was just emerging from the lane. Its engine gave a belch and the car turned onto the road. It began to kangaroo along behind them. Clearly it wasn't the car it had once been, but it was there. Kev was roaring at Stick and Stick turned around.

"What?"

"Just keep on going," yelled George.

"Where to?" shouted Stick.

"Anywhere that looks like a town," George yelled back.

He put his head down and concentrated on pedaling. If they got to a town, they could find a police station, a policeman—anybody. After all, they had the kid with them now and her picture had been on TV. They wouldn't have to do any explaining, would they? He divided his mind between rehearsing odd French phrases he'd come across in Mr. Martin's class and paying attention to what was going on behind them. The odd French phrases weren't much use. He could tell people he liked swimming till he was blue in the face and it wouldn't explain what they were doing with a kidnapped kid.

As for what was going on behind them, that was more reassuring. The car would lurch about a hundred yards at a time, splutter a bit, and stop. Then he would hear the engine rev and catch again for another hundred-yard lurch. The unnerving thing was that every so often it would seem to ignore all the stuff in its tank and behave like a normal car. One of the times that happened, the guy ended up no more than ten yards behind them. George looked back through the windshield at the driver and wished he hadn't. Even through the smoked glass he could see the expression on his face. Suddenly his feet on the pedals seemed to be going twice as fast. The car spluttered, coughed, and died. Stick's voice floated back to him faintly.

"A town."

George breathed a sigh of relief as they left the car standing and the town came into view.

"Looks pretty nice," said Tub beside him. "Just a village really."

George spared him a glance. "This is no time for sightseeing," he said. "Anyway, I thought you didn't like sightseeing."

"Churches," said Tub. "Churches are boring."

"Not that last one," said George.

"There are people with funny clothes on dancing in the square," said Tub.

"We'll come back another day and take pictures," George said. "Can you see any policemen?"

"Nope," said Tub. "Just all these people . . ."

"I know," said George, "dancing."

They braked their bikes at the edge of the square and got off.

"Do you think we've lost him?" said Stick.

"I think he's going to have to walk the rest of the way," said George.

"What now?" said Julia.

"We find the police station," said George.

"What does it look like?" said Julia.

"How should I know?" said George. "What's French for 'police'?"

"Zhon darm," said Kev.

"Right," said George. "Spread out and ask people where it is."

"How?" said Tub.

"Just say what Kev said," said George. "What was it, Kev?"

"Zhon darm," said Kev carefully.

There were a lot of people around the square watching the dancing. It seemed to be some kind of folk festival. There was a fiddler and a guitarist and a man playing an accordion and all these people all dressed up, dancing away in the middle of the square. The men were wearing black trousers and short jackets with brass buttons on them and big black hats. The women were wearing embroidered black dresses with white aprons. They had what looked like lace pancakes on their heads.

"Kev," said George, "you and Stick go around one way and we'll go around the other and the first person to score a hit shouts."

"Shouts what?" said Kev.

"Shouts anything," said George, "only not in French," he added. You had to be careful with this strange talent of Kev's.

George, Tub, and Julia started out around the square shouting "zhon darm" at people. Mostly they just smiled and said things like "ong glaze" to each other and "foo"—as if they'd suddenly come across a bad smell. They had no luck. Neither had Kev and Stick when they met at the other end of the square.

"What now, George?" said Stick.

George ran a hand through his hair and looked around. Just behind them was a sidewalk café. France seemed to be full of sidewalk cafés. There was an old man in a dark blue shirt and a beret sitting at a table reading a newspaper and drinking a glass of wine. Next to him was a stick and one of those electric wheelchairs. George wondered if the person who owned the wheelchair had gone for a walk. The old man had the paper held up in front of him and there, staring out at George, was a picture of Tamarind. George turned to grab her and she wasn't there. The gorilla was empty. It gazed at him soulfully.

"Where is she?" said George.

Kev glanced around. "She wanted to dance," he said.

"What?" said George, and looked toward the center of the square. There, in the middle of the dancers, was Tamarind, holding out her frilly dress and skipping in and out of all these people with funny clothes on. She seemed to be having a great time. People were calling to her and clapping—urging her on. Irresponsible people.

"Don't any of these people read the newspapers?" said George.

He turned to the old man with the paper and said the one word of French he was good at—"*pardon*"—and snatched it out of the old man's hands. Waving it and pointing to the picture, he ran into the crowd of dancers and grabbed Tamarind. She kept on dancing, dragging George after her, and he found himself skipping through the dancers, wondering what the French for 'help' was.

"Mayday," he yelled. "Look, it's her. Mayday."

After all, it was supposed to be international. He'd learned that in the scouts, though he had a feeling it was something to do with the sea.

The crowd carried on clapping even when the old man broke through and started hobbling around on his stick, waving his other arm and shouting at George. He distracted George's attention. He started waving the stick around now. He had a pretty good aim. It was just his balance that wasn't reliable.

It was only when Stick grabbed George's arm and

started roaring in his ear that he realized another sound had been added to the music. It was a spluttering, coughing sound made by an engine in distress, and as George watched, horrified, the big black car lurched into the middle of the square and stopped with a final belch that seemed to say it had had enough. There was a faint stream of smoke coming from the hood and out of the gas tank bubbled a curious froth tinged with yellow. The smell wasn't too great either. George looked around to see if anybody was saying "foo." He waved the newspaper under the nose of the accordionist just as he was closing the bellows on a crashing chord. The paper slotted itself neatly into the bellows and waved around a bit. The man with the accordion didn't look too pleased. Granddad was still after him with the stick.

"It's her," said George, fending off the blows. "Look," and he yanked Tamarind to a standstill.

"Oh, look," she said, and he turned to find the guy in the leather jacket bearing down on them. He gave up in despair. He knew now what people meant when they talked about the language barrier. By now, with the accordionist out of action and the car all over the square, George was the only one who was still dancing—thanks to Granddad's stick.

"Come on," he yelled to the rest.

He kept a tight hold of Tamarind and barged his

way through the crowd. The accordionist was extracting the newspaper from his accordion. He looked at the front page for a moment, then turned and looked at Tamarind as she flew past, caught in George's grip, her feet hardly touching the ground. George was too busy to notice. He crammed Tamarind back into the gorilla.

"Where are we going now?" she said to George. "I like this."

George looked at her in disgust. The crowd had gathered around the man in the leather jacket, wedging him in. They could see him pointing at his car, at the newspaper, at them. What on earth was he up to? The crowd surged toward them. It didn't look friendly.

"He's got them on his side," said George in disbelief. "Let's get out of here."

They were on the bikes and pedaling fast before they noticed that what looked like the whole village was following them—in cars, on bikes, on those funny little motor scooters the French go in for, and on foot—all of them. The people on foot were in the lead. The bikes were coming a close second, but the cars were getting snarled up, all trying to get out of the village at once. Several of the leading drivers got out and started arguing with each other, and then none of the rest could get out of the square. The old man with the beret was in the wheelchair now. He looked as if he was yelling at the bikes to get out of the way. If they didn't, he just swept the opposition aside with his stick as his wheelchair plowed its way through the crowd.

"They're mad," said George as Kev overtook him.

"Foo," said Kev on the way past.

"What?" said George.

"Foo," Kev called back. "It means 'mad'."

So that's what it meant, thought George. Even he had known what "ong glaze" had meant. Charming, he thought.

"*Charmant*," he muttered, dredging up another French word from the recesses of his memory.

They were leaving the pedestrians behind, but some of the bikes were beginning to make ground and, looking back, he saw one or two cars manage to edge their way out of the village. Granddad in the electric wheelchair wasn't doing too badly either.

The road out of the village was really twisty. They slowed down to try to get the lay of the land.

"We've got to try to get back to Auray," George said.

"There aren't any signposts," said Julia.

Stick was standing up on the pedals of his bike, looking over the hedge at the side of the road. "It's over there," he said.

The rest craned their necks to see. Stick was right. The road they had taken must have brought them around almost in a full circle, and there across the fields was the road to Auray. They could see bunting fluttering in the breeze. That must be the junction where they had left the road when they were following the car. It didn't look too far, but if the road went on twisting like this, they would never get there before the mob from the village caught up with them. They came around a sharp bend and suddenly there was a gap in the hedge just made for them. That was all they needed.

"Okay, the mountain bikes," George yelled. "Cross country. Toot sweet."

His French was getting quite good.

They plowed off the road and into the fields. George looked admiringly at Stick. Height could be useful at times. Even the yellow T-shirt looked good for a moment.

"Okay, Tamarind?" he shouted as Kev flashed past.

"This is much better than my other kidnapping," she shouted back. She was cuddling the gorilla.

Kev turned around to her. "That's nice," he said, and hitched her higher on his back.

They seemed to be getting along fine.

The bikes were terrific on this ground, even if they did make your teeth rattle a bit. The gorilla sounded as if it were playing the castanets. There was a bad moment when they heard the cars and bikes on the road behind them, but the sounds died away. With the twisting of the road the mob must have thought they were still in pursuit. They pedaled on furiously. Every so often they saw the flash of cars behind the hedge that lined the road, but it looked as if they were going to make it to the junction first. The bunting got nearer and nearer. The only thing was, the nearer they got to the junction, the closer they got to the road the mob was on, where it swung back to meet the junction for Auray. George couldn't feel his legs anymore. They seemed to belong to somebody else. The sound of engines on the road was getting louder again. It was going to be neck and neck. Then another sound drowned out the car engines. At first he couldn't make out where it was coming from—till he looked up.

"A helicopter," he muttered. "That's all we need."

The helicopter came swooping across the fields, flattening the grass as it came. Tamarind was squealing with delight.

"Ignore it," shouted George. "Look at the cars."

The hedges had thinned out and they could see the line of cars hurtling down the road to cut them off, horns blaring, people leaning out of windows, shouting. They had been spotted at last. Ahead they could see where the field joined the road. Bunting stretched across it and people were lined along the edge of the field. The shadow of the helicopter fell

across them, and the down draft nearly knocked them off balance. The leading car was almost at the crossroads. They could see the faces of the people by the side of the field turn toward them, turn up to the helicopter, turn back toward the cars. They were approaching the road just where it swept down the hill to Auray, the place where they had cut off past the barrier when they were following the car. Bikes and cars homed in on the same point. They were still ahead, but only just.

George made up his mind. He turned his bike deliberately toward the road the cars were coming down.

"Make for the junction, you guys," he yelled. "Go for it, Kev."

The helicopter roared overhead, and he didn't catch what Kev yelled back. He was concentrating. He had to take the junction where it met the road the cars were on, and there was a barrier in his way. He thought it was the one that was already broken, which should make it easier. The last thing he saw as he crashed through the barrier was Stick sweeping through the bunting with Kev close behind. People leapt back as Tub and Julia followed, and George caught a glimpse of Stick taking off down the hill, bunting streaming—a yellow blur on a bike.

George braked right in the middle of the road and shut his eyes, mainly because there was a line of cars approaching him faster than he liked the look of. There was a screeching of brakes, a torrent of French, and then a roaring filled his ears and he thought maybe braking across the middle of the road hadn't been such a good idea, even if it did stop them.

He opened his eyes. He was still alive. He was glad of that for a moment—till he saw Granddad. His wheelchair was perched on the back of a low truck and he was waving his stick at George again. Threatening, you could call it. Other people were getting out of their cars. They did not look friendly. There seemed to be a good deal of cheering and roaring going on somewhere. George didn't stop to find out where. He wheeled his bike around and was off down the hill to Auray before Granddad could get at him.

Faces flashed past him as he swept down the hill. The road was lined with people. Ahead in the distance he could see Stick in the lead, yellow T-shirt fluttering and the bunting streaming out behind him. Kev was a close second with Tamarind bobbing around on his back and the gorilla grinning like something demented. As they passed, the crowd roared and clapped and then sort of trailed off as they got a good look at Kev. Tub and Julia were just in front now, but George passed them easily. Somewhere or other he had lost contact with the pedals of the bike. He hurtled down the hill, out of control. It wasn't his fault that he couldn't stop. He noticed with passing interest that Jenny was right about the river. The tide was in and the water was up to the edge of the square.

He was on Kev's heels now. He could see Tamarind's face quite clearly. She was singing again. It mesmerized him for a moment, and he swerved just in time to avoid hitting them. Kev's bike wobbled, and George turned briefly to check that they were all right. That was a mistake. When he turned back he'd almost run into Stick. The square rushed toward him. It was crammed with people, all yelling. Too late, he found the brakes. His front wheel touched Stick's back one just before he and the bike parted company. George felt himself sailing through the air. He caught an upside-down glimpse of Jenny's face just before he hit the water, then something yellow and skinny and trailing bunting fell on him, closely followed by a gorilla.

Things were a bit confused after that. George remembered sitting up in the water and saying, "Crazy place to put a river."

He remembered Stick clutching him, his eyes shining, and saying, "They cheered me all the way down the hill."

He remembered Tub and Julia braking at the very edge of the water and looking pleased with themselves until a truck, its brakes squealing, swerved to a stop behind them. Its tailgate clattered onto the cobblestones and Granddad and the wheelchair slid gently off the back. It caught them behind the knees and deposited them in the river. Granddad's wheelchair slid slowly in to join them. Luckily he seemed to have lost his stick.

"Won't do the electrics any good," said Tub, looking at the wheelchair.

George located Jenny. She was sitting at the sidewalk café by the river, and she looked as if she were going to say something George would rather not hear.

"You told us to meet you back here if we got separated," he said.

Tamarind had scrambled out of the gorilla and was trying to squeeze the water out of her kidnap dress.

"My frills are all wet," she said.

Julia hadn't said anything, which was odd. George looked at her. She had a smile on her face. It didn't seem to be the right expression for Julia under the circumstances. He followed her eyes. The gorilla was floating gently down the river on its back, grinning up at the sky and trailing bunting in its wake.

"Want me to rescue it?" he said.

The smile vanished. "You dare, George Aitken," said Julia. "You just dare."

But the thing he remembered most of all was the helicopter landing in the middle of the square. It caused quite a sensation, and a lot more people ended up in the river. George had nothing against the river. It wasn't very deep and it wasn't very cold, but it was a bit choppy and it was definitely getting overcrowded. He got to his feet and water poured out of him. The helicopter blades stopped whirling and the river settled down. Somebody got out of the helicopter—the man in the leather jacket. He was followed by a policeman. Thank goodness they've caught him, George remembered thinking as Tamarind splashed out of the water toward the man in the leather jacket, looked up at him, and said, "Daddy!"

George felt his legs go weak,and sank slowly back into the water. There were worse places to be, he thought. That was just before several hundred cyclists came steaming over the horizon and hurtled down the hill into the square. The crowd went mad—even those in the water.

Aitken, George
Papillon sur Mer

16

After that, it was as if somebody had announced a short intermission for pandemonium. People began wading out of the water toward the square. Not that there was much room for them. Children clambered over the helicopter unchecked. The police had deserted it. Even the driver had deserted it. They and about ten million others were clustered around a guy in a yellow T-shirt who had come crashing down the hill with the hundreds of other cyclists. The Tour de France had arrived. Everybody was shouting and waving their arms around, especially the guy in the yellow T-shirt.

"What's going on?" said Tub.

"It's the Tour de France," said Stick. "They're celebrating."

"Oh, that race," said Julia. She seemed quite happy. The gorilla had sunk.

"That guy doesn't look too pleased," said Kev.

"What guy?" Stick said.

"The one who's looking at you," Kev said. "The one in the yellow T-shirt."

As they watched, the guy in the yellow T-shirt started to wade into the water toward them.

"What have I done?" said Stick. "I've never seen that guy in my life before."

George looked from Stick in his cycling helmet and yellow T-shirt to the cyclist—in his cycling helmet and yellow T-shirt—and a thought occurred to him.

"If I were you, Stick," he said, "I'd make myself scarce."

"I haven't done anything," said Stick, but you could tell he was worried the way he was untangling himself from his bike and leaping up and down.

"Get Jenny," said Kev. "She'll talk at him for you."

Stick leapt off in the direction of the café. Tub, Kev, and Julia followed him. So did the guy in the yellow T-shirt.

George decided to stay where he was. He had things to think about, and it was more peaceful in the water now. It was only he and Granddad left, and Granddad was no problem—not now that he'd lost his stick. He was just sitting there in his wheelchair—well, not *just* sitting there. He was shouting a lot and throwing his arms around, but so was everybody else.

A faint screeching sound drew George's attention, and he looked up. Over the hill came a truck laden with folk dancers. They hung over the sides, on the doors. The guitarist was clinging to the roof of the cab with one hand and waving his guitar with the other. The accordionist was giving it everything he'd gotten from somewhere in the back of the truck. Somebody in the crowd was shaking up one of those big bottles of champagne. There was a small explosion and a fountain of spray shot into the air. The café was doing a roaring trade. Tamarind was dancing on Jenny's table. So where was "daddy"?

"I want to talk to you," said a voice.

George looked up. Question answered. It was the guy in the leather jacket. George made a break for it, but he didn't stand a chance. A hand on his collar yanked him back. He felt cold with fear—or maybe it was sitting in the water again that gave him that creepy feeling.

"Where are you going?" the guy said. "The police?"

Fear turned to confusion.

"The police?" he said. "You're the one who brought the police." A thought occurred to him. "Are you really her dad?" he said.

"Yeah."

Okay, thought George, he could say that, but what about the kid's description of her dad?

"I thought you weren't big any longer," George said.

The guy crouched down beside him. He didn't seem to mind getting wet, but then, it was a hot day.

"Don't you start," he said. "I get enough of that from my manager."

"What?" said George.

"Going on about how big I used to be."

"Sorry," said George. Maybe he was out of his mind.

"That's why I did it," the guy said.

"Did what?" said George.

"Kidnapped Tamarind."

"But you're her dad," said George. "How can you kidnap your own kid?"

The guy looked shocked. "You don't think I'd let anybody else kidnap her, do you?"

George looked at him. He looked quite sane, but you never knew.

"Why did you kidnap your own kid?" said George. He felt, he really felt he had to get this straight.

"Publicity," said the guy.

"Oh," said George. "Right. Of course."

He *was* out of his mind.

The guy was looking at him very closely.

"You don't know who I am, do you?" he said.

George didn't answer at once. It was tricky. Maybe he thought he was Napoleon—or Popeye—or a bunch of grapes. He began to wonder where Granddad's stick had gone to.

The guy sighed. "Mud sticks," he said.

It sounded like something Tub's mom would say. George started to feel around in the water for Granddad's stick.

"Can't argue with that," he said. You had to humor madmen, agree with them.

The guy shook his head. "See what I mean. You're too young."

There were two ways you could look at that. Either he hated young people, in which case George had had it, or he was going to let George get a bit older. Then a thought occurred to him. Tamarind's tour T-shirt, the one that looked dirty—all those splashes of mud. Her saying her dad used to be really big. Saying "My dad sings."

"Mudd Styx," he said.

The guy brightened up. "You *have* heard of me."

George nodded. "My mom's got some old records of yours. She says you used to be —" He stopped.

The guy was looking depressed again. "Really

173

big," he said. "I know. That's why I pulled the kidnap stunt. Tamarind was perfectly safe, you know. She was with me all the time."

"But how did you get her to go along with it?" George said. "I mean, if she'd told anybody . . ." Then he remembered she had told him and he hadn't believed her.

"I got her this dress," said the guy. "Her mom always dresses her in jeans and T-shirts and she hates it. She likes these frilly things. So I got her one and told her if she didn't say a word about not really being kidnapped, she could wear the dress."

George shook his head. Even he found it hard working that one out.

"It didn't work," he said.

"Didn't it?"

George felt really sorry for him.

"She calls it her kidnap dress. They'll ask her questions, you know."

"Tamarind hardly ever answers questions," said the guy. "She asks a lot though." He paused. "All I needed was a few days' good publicity, then I was going to rescue her and make the headlines as a hero."

"But you took her on the ferry yourself," said George. "Weren't you afraid someone would recognize you?"

Tamarind's dad gave him a look. "If people still

recognized me, I wouldn't have had to kidnap her. I wouldn't have needed the publicity."

"Oh, right," said George. "Sorry."

"Besides, the kidnapping was staged for after we got off the ferry."

"Look, Mr. Styx," said George.

"Call me Mudd."

"Look, Mudd," said George, and felt really stupid. "She knew you were kidnapping her—pretending to kidnap her."

Mudd nodded. "I had to tell her," he said. "She asks a lot of questions. She's like her mom."

George had a mental picture of a grown-up Tamarind.

"What's her mom going to say?" he said.

Mudd turned white. "She's gone to a health spa for a week," he said. "They don't allow them to have newspapers or TV. It's supposed to be relaxing. I thought by the time she came out, I'd be a hero and really—"

"Big?" said George.

"Big," said Mudd.

"I saw you, you know," said George. "When you took her out of one car and put her in another. In that parking lot. I was in a bus."

He looked even more depressed. "Don't seem to have managed it very well, do I?"

"Oh, I don't know," said George. "I mean, you got

TV coverage and the papers. They even sent out a helicopter."

Mudd obviously needed encouragement, but that wasn't the right thing to say. He scratched his head. "I never thought they'd do that," he said. "Send out a helicopter. I feel terrible about that. They need those for real emergencies."

George thought back to Kev and the sailing lessons and the helicopter coming to the rescue. "They weren't doing too much anyway," he said. "Don't worry about the helicopter."

Mudd wasn't listening. "Can you imagine what's going to happen when they find out?" he said. "They'll probably put me in prison. I don't know what Tamarind's mom is going to say."

"You haven't told the police, then?" said George.

He looked surprised.

"No," he said. "I was too worried about Tamarind. I had no idea where you were taking her. I just got hold of the police and they sent the helicopter. My French isn't very good."

George thought for a moment. "Don't tell them, then."

"What?"

"Stick to your original plan," said George. "What was it anyway?"

Mudd blushed. He really didn't make a very good criminal.

"I was going to say I'd had a note telling me to be at

that farm with money. Then I was going to say I'd burst in and rescued her. The kidnappers would have to get away, of course."

"Of course," said George. Secretly he thought the guy probably saw too many movies, but that was his problem.

"Stick to that, then, Mudd," he said, and paused. Had he gotten that right?

"What about you guys?" said Mudd.

George shrugged. "That's no problem. We just tell the truth." What a strange thing for him to say, he thought. "After all," he went on, "as far as we were concerned, when we got to that house, you were the kidnapper. We needn't have seen you on the boat at all. We'll just leave that part out. I can put in the part about seeing the car, and that fits with us following it."

"What about the church?" said Mudd.

George thought. "We keep that out as well," he said. "You have to be selective about the truth. It can upset people. Why did you go there anyway?"

Mudd shrugged. "Tamarind wanted to," he said. "They have this festival when they decorate that church, and I told her about it."

"That's a bit crazy," said George.

Mudd nodded. "Anyway, everybody was down here waiting for the Tour de France. The rest of the town was deserted."

"Apart from us," said George.

"Apart from you," said Mudd. "What were you doing there anyway?"

"We were with a social worker who likes old churches," said George.

"Bossy?" said Mudd.

George thought. "No, not bossy, but she talks a lot once she gets going."

Mudd grinned. He looked quite nice really—not crazy at all.

"You'll really go along with all this?" he said.

George thought of Jenny and the churches, Sharon and the Friends of the Animals, Tamarind and her perpetual "whys?," his mom and the state of his bedroom. There was no doubt about it, women were a problem. It wasn't the thought of prison that was getting Mudd down. It was what Tamarind's mom would say.

"Why make trouble for yourself?" he said.

Mudd was looking puzzled. "You don't think what I've told you is really weird?"

George stood up. Water poured off him—again.

"You haven't met Kev," he said.

Mudd stood up too. "And the rest? They'll go along with it as well? I mean, there wasn't really a kidnapping at all."

George shrugged. "They won't care. I had exactly the same problem with a cat. That kind of thing can lead to a load of trouble if you're not careful."

George took hold of Granddad's wheelchair and wheeled him out of the water while he told Mudd about the cat that wasn't in Mr. Martin's room. Granddad was no bother. He had gone to sleep in the sun.

They forced their way through the cyclists, the folk dancers, the spectators, and the "zhon darms," using Granddad in his wheelchair as a battering ram. He slept peacefully. He wasn't that young, George thought, and he'd had a busy day.

Eventually they got to the café. Tub was eating pancakes again, and Julia and Kev were arguing about the gorilla.

"I liked it," Kev was saying.

Stick was trying to hide behind Jenny, who was doing a good job calming down the cyclist in the yellow T-shirt. George could see how your view of Jenny's talking could change, depending on whether or not she was on your side.

"What's French for 'help,' George?" said Stick.

George looked at Mudd.

"Must be *m'aidez*, mustn't it?" said Mudd.

George was pleased. "That's what I thought," he said. "Mayday, Stick."

"Well, mayday me, then," said Stick. "This guy thinks I tried to mess up his bike race."

"That's ridiculous," said Tub. "We got here long before the bike race. We were nowhere near them."

Jenny broke off talking to the cyclist in the yellow T-shirt. "That's the point, Tub," she said. "Stick came racing down that hill in a yellow T-shirt and everybody thought it was the Tour de France leader in his yellow jersey. I mean, you even have a helmet."

"I can't help what people think," said Stick. "It wasn't my fault."

"That's why they all cheered you," said Julia.

"Till they saw Kev and the gorilla," said Tub through a mouthful of pancakes. "They stopped then. Nobody thought Kev and the gorilla were in the Tour de France."

"Forget the Tour de France," said George.

"It's all right for him to say that," said Stick to Tub.

"Who's that?" said Jenny, looking at Granddad.

"Some old guy," said George. "It's okay. He's lost his stick."

"What?" said Stick.

"What?" said Mudd.

George hung on to his patience. There were too many sticks around here.

"Look," he said to Stick, "let Jenny explain to this guy that you weren't trying to mess up his race, and come over here. I've got something to tell you."

Jenny looked at Stick. "You're right, George. I'd do better without him. He keeps muttering about kidnappers."

But Stick was pointing at Mudd. "That's him," he

said. "That's the kidnapper. Where's the kid?"

Tamarind leapt off the table behind Stick and into Mudd's arms.

"Daddy," she said. "Where's my monkey?"

"Really, Stick," said Jenny. "Don't make things worse than they are already."

"Ignore him," said George. "He landed on his head when he fell off the bike."

He reached out a hand and yanked Stick out of harm's way.

"Come on, you guys," he said to the rest.

Tub brought his pancakes with him. Julia had absentmindedly wheeled Granddad along. They sat down at a table as far away from Jenny as they could, and George embarked on the explanation of the kidnapping. It wasn't easy. He ran through the story once, just for openers. He took his time about it and went into detail. Then he sat back and waited for the questions.

"Where's my monkey?" said Tamarind.

"Gorilla," said Stick.

Mudd looked at Kev.

"Not me, it's another one she means," Kev said.

"It was supposed to be a panda," Julia said.

"I thought you hated it anyway," said Tub.

It wasn't what George had expected.

"Isn't anybody going to ask any questions?" he said.

"What about?" said Tub.

"The kidnapping," said George.

"You just said there wasn't one," said Stick.

"There wasn't—not really," said George.

"No point in asking questions about it, then, is there?" said Julia.

George looked at Kev. "Kev?"

"What?"

"Have you any questions?"

"Yeah," said Kev.

George breathed a sigh of relief. It hadn't seemed real, them not hammering him with questions.

"Well?" said George.

"Well what?" said Kev.

"The question you wanted to ask," said George.

Kev's eyebrows drew together. "Oh, yeah," he said. "What are we going to tell Mr. Martin about the first aid kit?"

Mudd looked at George. "Are they always like this?" he said.

"No," said George. "Well, yes. It depends what you mean."

"Never mind," said Mudd. "It suits me fine."

Granddad woke up and started yelling again.

"What's he saying, Kev?" said George.

"Something about a stick," said Kev.

"Does he speak French?" said Mudd.

"No," said George, "but he understands it—sometimes."

"What was that about a first aid kit?"

George looked slightly embarrassed. "Oh, we know where it is, all right," he said. "It isn't as if we've lost it exactly."

"Where is it, then?" said Mudd.

"In your gas tank," said George.

"George," said Jenny's voice behind him. "The police want to talk to you and to Mr. . . . I'm sorry, it sounded like *steaks*."

"Styx," said Mudd. "Call me Mudd."

Jenny's face lit up. "*The* Mudd Styx," she said. "I've got all your records!"

She and Mudd went off, and George and the rest trailed Tamarind after them. They decided against taking Granddad. He was too noisy.

"*The* Mudd Styx," said Julia. "How many does she think there are?"

"Look, Tamarind," George was saying. "If anybody asks you any questions, don't answer. You can sing and dance as much as you like, but don't answer questions."

"What's that mean?" said Tamarind.

"What?" said George.

"Answer?" said Tamarind.

George thought she would be okay.

Aitken, George
Papillon sur Mer

17

"kay, who's going to do the talking?" said Tub.

They all looked at George.

"My French is rotten," said George.

He was beginning to feel a bit apprehensive. The story had sounded okay when he and Mudd had talked about it. It wasn't looking so good now that he actually had to try it out. Still, his French *was* rotten, and it would be a French policeman, so they couldn't expect a lot from him.

The policeman spoke English—sort of—which George thought was a lousy trick. He was throwing kids off the helicopter when George and the rest arrived, and none too gently either. George and Mudd looked at each other.

"You go first," said George generously.

But it was Jenny who went first.

"As the person in charge of these children, I suggest you deal with me. . . ." she began, and she was off.

"Who's she calling children?" said Julia.

"Great, isn't she?" said Kev, grinning.

George was inclined to agree with him. Even when she kept firing questions at him like "Why didn't you tell me what was happening, George?" and "Is this correct, George?" and "What monkey?" George didn't mind. She was doing a terrific job. The policeman looked quite relieved when it was Mudd's turn. Mudd was pretty good too. By the time he'd finished the story he and George had rehearsed, even George half believed it. After all, it was half true. Any time he seemed to be struggling, Jenny dived in to protect the underdog.

"Really, Officer," she said when Mudd got to the tricky bit about the ransom note, "I do think you should understand how upset Mr. Styx must have been."

The policeman lit another cigarette. He was chain-smoking and the smell was terrible.

"But whare ees zees not?" he said.

"Where is what not?" said Jenny.

"Zee not ee got," said the policeman.

Julia was doubled up. Stick clamped a hand over her mouth and she bit him.

"Ow," said Stick.

"How?" said the policeman.

"Oh, the note," said Jenny.

"Did the monkey eat it, Daddy?" said Tamarind.

"Ah," said the policeman, "and whare ees ze minki?"

"It drowned," said Julia.

"I really couldn't tell you where the note is," said Mudd, which was perfectly true.

"And zee man, zee keednupper," said the policeman. "You can tell me what ee looked like?"

"I'm afraid I can't really," said Mudd. "The confusion . . . I was interested only in my daughter's safety."

"Perhaps zee leetle girl," said the policeman. He turned to Tamarind and smiled. "Oo was it oo keednupped you?" he said.

Tamarind smiled back. "Daddy," she said.

George held his breath. The policeman smiled again. Tamarind gave a little dance and fluffed out her frills.

"Then *he* put me in the monkey," she said, pointing at George. "I liked that. It was just like Red Riding Hood and the wolf. Can I sing now?" she said to George.

"Sure," said George. "Go ahead."

Tamarind began to sing. It wasn't any better than the last time. The policeman winced. He turned to Mudd.

"Ow can we find ze keednupper if we do not know what ee looks like?" he said.

Mudd relaxed. "Don't bother," he said.

"*Pardon?*" the policeman said—the French way.

"I mean, I'm happy to have my daughter back. That's all I care about."

The policeman looked at Tamarind. The noise was terrible.

"You are?" he said. He looked puzzled. "And zees children? You do not want to priss chirges?"

"What?" said Mudd.

"Priss chirges," said the policeman.

"Kev," said George, "what's he saying?"

Kev looked blank. "I don't think it's French," he said.

"Priss chirges," said Tub. "He's asking if Mudd wants to press charges against us. What a nerve."

George looked at him. "How did you know that's what he was saying?"

Tub swallowed the last of his pancakes. "My mom watches *'Allo 'Allo,*" he said.

"No, no," Mudd was saying. "Not at all. These children were doing only what they thought was right. When you think about it, they were very brave."

Julia had been getting really mad. She hated it when people called her a child. She cheered up a bit at being called brave.

A crowd had gathered around, mainly, George thought, to find out who was killing somebody. Tamarind kept on singing. She loved an audience. George saw the accordionist from the village. He still had the newspaper. He shouted something over his shoulder and the crowd of folk dancers appeared and began to bombard the policeman with French. They could hear a whisper go around the crowd—"mod steaks, mod steaks." The accordionist started to play a tune and several of the crowd started singing. The guy with the guitar was shoved forward and held his guitar out to Mudd. Mudd looked around. The policeman was invisible behind the folk dancers.

"Oh, go on," said Jenny. "Sing my favorite."

"What's that?" said Mudd.

"The one he's playing," said Jenny, smiling at the accordionist. "'Tight Corner, Tight Squeeze.'"

Mudd grinned at George. "Right on," he said. "Tamarind?"

"What, Daddy?"

"Pack it in."

Tamarind packed it in. George was impressed. Mudd leapt onto a table, swiveled his hips a bit, and struck a chord on the guitar. The crowd gathered

around quieted down. He gave them a few more chords, a couple of swivels, a toss of the head, and launched into the song. Tamarind wasn't the only one who liked an audience.

The whole thing turned into quite a party. Somebody found the P.A. system they had been using for the Tour de France. The TV crews shuffled up with their cameras and the journalists gathered around. Even the cyclists wandered up. They'd had their moment of glory. Now it was Mudd's turn. Publicity, thought George, he's certainly getting that. Jenny was bobbing around, swinging her hair.

"You okay?" said George.

"Okay?" she said. "Wait till I tell Giles. Mudd Styx live in concert. And I thought he'd given it all up."

"His manager will be pleased," said George.

"What?" said Jenny.

"Oh, nothing," said George. "Just another good deed done."

"I thought you got thrown out of the scouts," said Jenny.

"I did," said George, "and they don't know what they're missing."

It was late by the time they got back to the camp. Mr. Martin was jumping up and down.

"Where have you been?" he said. "I was getting worried."

"Oh, Giles," said Jenny, and George and the rest left her and went to bed. It had been a tiring day. It wasn't till the next morning that they found out they were heroes. Jenny had really done her stuff. Sharon came and sat beside them at breakfast. "It doesn't matter that it wasn't the kidnapper," she said. "I think it was really brave of you to go after him like that, George. A poor, helpless little child and you went to her rescue. I'm proud of you, George, and I've spoken to the sailing instructor. He's going to let you back into water sports."

"Just as well," said Mr. Martin's voice behind them. "You're even more of a menace on dry land."

"Oh, Mr. Martin, how can you say that?" said Sharon.

"It's easy," he said. "I've had lots of practice with this bunch."

George dragged his mind away from the picture of Tamarind as a poor, helpless little child. "You've got a suspicious nature, Mr. Martin," he said.

"Goes with the job," said Mr. Martin. "Do you know anything about an electric wheelchair?"

They all looked blank. They were good at looking blank.

"Yes, I thought you did," said Mr. Martin. "Never mind, that pop singer is going to pay for the repair."

"Mudd Styx," said Julia.

Mr. Martin grunted and turned away.

"He's jealous," said Julia.

"Nothing of the sort," Mr. Martin said over his shoulder. "It's just not my taste in music."

"He *is* jealous," said Julia, satisfied.

"So, this afternoon I'll give you a lesson in tacking," Sharon was saying.

George smiled gratefully. Brave, she'd said he was. It was nearly as good as "my hero." Maybe she would let him keep his badge after all. Maybe she would give him a better one—one really high up in the genetic scale. A monkey maybe. Maybe not a monkey. She drifted off in shades of blond.

"What a sap," said Julia. "You'll never last. Bet she's sent you packing by tomorrow."

"You're on," said George.

Aitken, George
Papillon sur Mer

18

Ｇeorge was really pleased that Sharon was taking
an interest in him—really pleased. It was just that
after a day and a half of her teaching him to sail, he
felt a bit worn out. His eyes kept drifting across the
water to where the rest of them were trying to see
how many windsurfing boards they could get
through before tomorrow. Tomorrow was the last
day of the vacation.

"Pay attention, George," Sharon said.

George looked at her. She was perfect. Maybe that
was it. Maybe he needed a bit of practice with imperfect before he could manage perfect. He knew

where he could get some practice with imperfect. He stood on the edge of the boat and thrust his arms out.

"George?" said Sharon. "What are you doing?"

George dived. Some things were impossible to explain. He surfaced in the middle of the ring of windsurfing boards and narrowly missed getting his head sliced off by Stick's board. They were fighting, as usual.

"Oh," said Julia. "You're back. Told you, didn't I? Did she throw you off the boat?"

George upended her board and climbed on.

"Okay," he said, "how do you work these things?"

After that things returned pretty much to normal.

Normal was interrupted a half hour later by shouts from the shore. They looked and saw Mr. Martin calling them in.

"What now?" said Tub.

They waded out of the water.

"That pop singer has come to see you," said Mr. Martin.

"Mudd Styx," said Julia, enjoying herself.

"Anyway, he's driven up in this really showy car," said Mr. Martin.

"Black, with smoked glass windows?" said George, suddenly remembering the gas tank.

"Silver," said Mr. Martin, "with gold trim and leopard-skin seats."

He had parked it outside the dining room. Jenny was with him. So was Tamarind. She was clutching a huge pink monkey.

"It isn't as nice as the other one," she said.

"I'll get my gran to make you one just like the other one," Julia said. "Ask your mom if she's got any old fur coats."

"What about the teeth?" said Tamarind. "Will it have teeth as well? I liked the teeth."

"She can't ask her mom for teeth," said Stick.

"Why not?" said Julia. "They'll probably be gold-plated. Look at that car."

Tub and Kev were wedged inside it, examining the controls.

"I just came to give you these," Mudd was saying. He was handing out a pile of white cards.

"What are they?" said George.

"Complimentary tickets," said Mudd. "Backstage passes and row A seats. My manager has arranged a date in London for the month after next—a comeback concert. The tickets are for you and your families—the concert and a champagne supper afterward at the Ritz."

"The Ritz?" said George. "That's quite extravagant, isn't it?"

Mudd shrugged. "No problem," he said. "I've got a tour of France arranged as well. I'm back in business."

George grinned. "Nothing to do with all that publicity, of course."

"Of course not," said Mudd, and winked. He turned to Jenny. "Would you like tickets too?"

Jenny hesitated. "Giles will be on vacation then," she said. "We're going to be awfully busy"—her eyes went to the sea below—"canoeing," she finished.

"All these vacations teachers get," Mudd said. "Talk about an easy life."

Mr. Martin unglued his eyes from Mudd's car. He looked as if he were about to leap for his throat.

"What happened to the other car—the black one?" George said as Jenny led Mr. Martin away.

He could hear Mr. Martin say, "Canoeing?"

"That car's really tacky," Jenny said. "I didn't like it, did you?"

Mudd was speaking. ". . . police thought it was very clever of the kidnapper to rent it under my name. They didn't even ask me to go to pick it up or anything."

"They didn't think it really was you, then?"

Mudd grinned. "Who would believe a thing like that?"

"Talk about luck," said George.

"And a bit of help from you guys," said Mudd. "Without you backing me up, all the luck in the world wouldn't have helped."

"Couldn't really do anything else," said George. "After all, we messed up your plans."

Luck, he was thinking, you really did make your own.

"My dad's got one just like this," Kev said, sticking his head out of the car window.

"What? Gold trim and leopard-skin seats?" said Stick.

"My manager chose it," said Mudd. "Thinks it's good for the image."

"Your dad's got a beat-up old Ford," said George.

"No, I mean the tape player," said Kev. "He got it last month. Never stops playing it. All the time he's driving."

"What kind of music?" said Mudd.

"Oh, it isn't music," said Kev. "He started this evening class and he has to play a tape every week. He just plays it and plays it all the time in the car. Says it's the only time he gets peace to listen to it."

"He wouldn't get much peace with you in the car," said Tub.

"He does," said Kev. "It puts me to sleep. Every time he plays it. It's hardly started and I'm asleep. It's amazing."

"Must be something to do with the voice," said Julia.

"What's on the tape?" said Stick. Something that could put Kev to sleep instantly could be useful.

"I don't know," said Kev. "I'm asleep."

"You must hear some of it," said Tub, "for it to put you to sleep in the first place."

"I don't know," said Kev. "It's just this voice—talking."

"Well, what's it saying, then?" said Stick.

"I don't know, do I?" said Kev. "It isn't even English."

Stick gave up, but George took up the challenge. "What is it, then, if it isn't English?"

"French," said Kev. "That's what his evening class is. French conversation."

George looked at Kev in wonder. "That's how you can understand bits of French," he said. "That voice must hypnotize you and you learn in your sleep."

"You need to have things dangling in front of your eyes to be hypnotized," said Julia.

"No, you don't," said Tub. "A voice can do it. My mom saw a program on TV about it. It's something to do with brain-wave patterns."

"So why doesn't it put his dad to sleep?" said Julia. "Or everybody else who listens to it? Why doesn't it put the whole class to sleep?"

"Kev must have very unusual brain-wave patterns," said Tub. "The voice must match up with your brain-wave patterns, Kev."

"I didn't know I had any brain-wave patterns," said Kev.

"I didn't know he had any brain waves," said Stick.

"I didn't know he had any brains," said Julia.

Well, well, George thought. You learn something new every day. Imagine Kev having brain waves.

"Thanks for the tickets," he said to Mudd.

"Oh, yeah, thanks," said Stick and the rest.

When they looked back, Stick thought they hadn't thanked Mudd enough. It was when they got home and Stick's mom was waiting at the school for them. She had the dog with her. The dog leapt for Stick and bit him.

"Maybe your gran can make a knapsack out of it," said George.

Julia groaned. "What's she going to say when she hears about the gorilla—panda, I mean."

"Well, it went out in style," said George. "Burial at sea. All that was missing was the flag."

"There was the bunting," said Stick.

"There you are, then," said George. "Who could ask for more?"

"Got it," said Stick.

"What?" said George.

"Hi, Mom," said Stick. "You like Mudd Styx, don't you?"

Julia cheered up. "How do you think Gran would like a night out at the Ritz," she said.

"Do they have French waiters at the Ritz?" said Kev.

"I suppose so," said Tub. "Why?"

"My dad could practice his French," Kev said.

George thought of his mom at the Ritz. She would love it. She liked Mudd Styx as well.

"Do you think they'll have those things at the Ritz?" said Tub.

"What things?" George said.

"Those pancake things. What do they call them?"

"Hey, Kev," said George. "What's French for 'pancakes'?"

"Krepps," said Kev, and looked surprised.

"So how do you ask for them?" said Tub. "In France I just pointed."

"It'll be easy," said George. "And if you get stuck, just shout mayday."

"What's that French for?" said Tub.

"Help!" said George.

About the author

Helen McCann writes books for children as a tribute to stories that made her laugh as a child. The characters in *What Do We Do Now, George?* and *What's French for "Help," George?* were inspired by her own two children.

A lecturer in law, Helen McCann enjoys music, reading, and painting. She lives in Scotland.

About the illustrator

Ellen Eagle has illustrated many novels and picture books, including the Magic Mysteries by Elizabeth Levy, *Tales of Tiddly* by Dolores Modrell, and *What Do We Do Now, George?* by Helen McCann.

She and her husband live in Glen Ridge, New Jersey.